4/13

The Final Gift

Kathleen McGlinchey

authorHOUSE®

AuthorHouse™
1663 Liberty Drive, Suite 200
Bloomington, IN 47403
www.authorhouse.com
Phone: 1-800-839-8640

First published by AuthorHouse   10/17/2008

ISBN: 978-1-4343-7221-5 (sc)

Printed in the United States of America
Bloomington, Indiana

This book is printed on acid-free paper.

To Matthew and Megan

Introduction

I was awakened on that cold, icy, February twenty-sixth morning by the sound of the telephone ringing. The first call was from the school phone chain, reporting that there would be no school due to icy road conditions. I had just snuggled back into bed when the phone rang again. This time, it was my older brother, Jack, calling to let me know that he and Ed, my eldest brother, were on their way to my sister Maureen's house, to take her to the hospital. She was having pains in her chest every time she took a breath. I jumped out of bed and told Jack that I would meet them in Detroit as soon as I could drive there.

Fortunately, the salt trucks had done their job on the roads, and in no time I had made the two-hour drive from Lansing, Michigan, to Detroit. I'm sure I drove at the maximum speed allowed. Even so, the trip seemed to take forever. I arrived at Harper Hospital at our rendezvous point, but Maureen was not checked in yet. I sat in the lobby and waited.

Within thirty minutes, Jack and Ed pulled up in Maureen's van. I ran to meet them and noticed that Maureen was lying flat on her back in the middle seat. Apparently, that was the most comfortable position for her. My brothers went to get the wheelchair while I kept her company. Her breathing was very shallow, almost as if she was afraid to take a deep breath.

She didn't appear to be the same person I had seen the day before. We had all gathered at her house on Sunday to celebrate her forty-seventh birthday. Today, her face was winced in pain. I tried to comfort her the best I could until Jack and Ed returned with the wheelchair. As they tried to take her from the car, as gently as they possibly could, she moaned and made her discomfort known. Even though she must have been in excruciating pain, she never screamed at any of us. She'd just say "Easy" or "Gentle." It's not possible for me to relate how I wanted to make it all go away. I hated to see her suffer.

After what seemed like an eternity, she was taken up to a room, and I followed. I think I was crying the entire time, although I tried not to let her see me. When she was settled in the room, I held her hand, and I said to her, "Maureen, if you get tired of all this and you want to go, you just go ahead and go."

She looked at me and said in her agony, "Are you kidding? I'm not going anywhere. I'm just offering this up to God." I was so relieved and glad that she thought I was kidding. It assured me that she was still going to fight. I really wasn't ready for her to be anyplace except with us.

We stayed with her for the rest of the day. The doctors gave her some pain medication and ran some tests. Like so many times before, we would know the results soon.

Beginnings

Early Heritage

I've often heard it said that we somehow choose the families in which we are born. If that's the case, I managed to pick a good one. My family was a big, first-generation, Irish Catholic family. While growing up with so many siblings, there was always someone to play with or annoy, as the case may be. Most importantly, there was always an abundance of love... plenty enough for everyone.

We owe our heritage to two amazing people, and the real story begins with them. My parents were born and raised in Ireland. My mother, Margaret Starr, was born on July 17, 1910, in Derrygoolin, Woodford, County Galway. Like most families during that time, they were dirt-poor. She had nine siblings. They lived on a farm and managed as best as they could. Her life during her nineteen years in Ireland consisted of tough, hard years. Like most children of her era, she finished school in the eighth grade. Formal school ended at that time because the children were needed to work on the farm.

Seeking a better life, at the age of nineteen, in 1929, she bravely walked away from the little village in Ireland, made her way to Liverpool, England, boarded a ship, and sailed to America. The journey took almost two weeks, and she was sick the entire time. She finally landed in New York, was cleared through customs, and then took a train to Detroit, where she had planned to meet her sister, Catherine, who had come to America a few years before. As she got off the train, obviously exhausted from her journey, she accidentally left her coat on the train and was greeted by late-fall Michigan weather. Fortunately, Catherine was there to rescue her with a warm coat.

Within a few days, Mom was hired as a nanny for a family. She always believed she was hired because she was an immigrant. In 1934, Margaret Starr became an American citizen.

It wasn't long before she met, dated, and became engaged to a guy named Patrick Scanlin. He told her that once they became engaged, he would take her back to Ireland. The engagement continued for some time, yet no trip to Ireland was scheduled. She became tired of waiting and went back to Ireland by herself in 1938. When she left Ireland after her visit, she had no idea it would be the last time she would see her parents and the last time she would go home to Ireland for twenty-five years.

Upon her return to America, she returned the engagement ring to Patrick because "If he couldn't keep a promise to take me to Ireland, how could he keep a marriage promise?" She began dating again and soon met Jack Langford. She was convinced this was "true love" and that she would marry Jack. On Mother's Day in 1940, she and Jack had a date planned, and Jack called and asked if his friend, Eddie McGlinchey, could join them. The three of them had a wonderful time, and Margaret was especially touched when Eddie brought her a bouquet of flowers. She soon realized that her "true love" was Eddie.

Approximately one year later, she walked down the aisle to become the wife and soulmate of Eddie McGlinchey. They were wed on April 26, 1940.

My father, Edward McGlinchey, was born in Skerry, Letterkenny, County Donegal, Ireland, on December 10, 1897. He, like Margaret, had a tough, hardworking, poor childhood. He left his parents and siblings in 1928 and sailed for America at the age of 31. He worked in Canada and then on a farm in the United States. Even though by that time America was in the midst of a depression, life was better than at any time in Ireland. He had a comfortable place to stay on the farm and was even earning a meager wage. In the mid-1930s, he made his way to Detroit, where he eventually landed a job with the Chrysler Corporation after working for the Packard Car Company.

The Children

I t wasn't long before Margaret and Eddie began producing some good, "thoroughbred" Irish children. First there was Edward Jr., who was born on May 27, 1941. Roseanne was next, on June 29, 1942. John, nicknamed Jack, followed two years later, on August 11, 1944. Pat followed on March 5, 1946, and Maureen on February 25, 1948. The "Irish twins" came next. Tom was born on January 16, 1950, and I was born the same year on my father's birthday, December 10. Finally, Margie (Margaret) was born on February 7, 1955.

When they were first married, Mom and Dad lived on Columbus Street in East Detroit. After Roseanne was born, they moved to Roseville, Michigan. They were never really crazy about the house, and Dad soon found a lot in Centerline where he would build his growing family a house with the help of some friends. Their negative instincts about the house in Roseville proved to be an omen of disaster. It became a place of great sadness on June 19, 1946.

The day had been very rainy. Mom was giving three month-old Pat a bath, and Ed, Jack, and Roseanne were out playing in the yard. Before long, Jack came running into the house, screaming that Roseanne had fallen into the ditch. Mom pulled Roseanne from the water-filled ditch, but it was too late. She had drowned.

Life afterwards was almost impossible for my mother. There was no end to her grief. There was no joy, only sadness and the responsibility of three other children. When she was desperate for relief from the despair, she recalls nodding off to sleep one night and seeing a vision of Roseanne being held in the arms of our Blessed Mother. She awoke with a great sense of peace and relief. They would persevere and carry on, determined to make life good again.

They moved out of the house in Roseville as quickly as they could. The new house in Centerline was only "roughed in," but it became their haven, a place to escape the bad memories. They planned to finish one room at a time and build new, pleasant memories there. It didn't take long. Their new daughter, "an angel from heaven" named Maureen, was born in February.

Centerline Memories

We had many happy memories in that house that became our home for almost thirty years. My favorite childhood recollections include the many Irish parties that we had. My relatives would come over, and Dad and his friend, Jim Ward, would break out their violins. Cornmeal would be thrown on the floor, and the legs and feet would fly. It always amazed me how they could spin around so fast and not get dizzy when they did their Irish set dancing. As I reflect on it now, there were subtle lessons being taught at these parties. Not only were we learning to absorb and respect our culture and heritage, but we were being taught the importance of family and the traits that bound us together. We were told countless times, through actions and words, that "there is nothing on earth more important than family." It was a message well taken. It was a prophecy that would become our source of strength in the years ahead.

Of course, in a family the size of ours, there are also many humorous stories relating to our childhood. I'm sure they weren't humorous at the time, but they are in the retelling. For example, when my brother Tom was about three years old, we were going to visit relatives on a Sunday afternoon. All of us were piled in the back seat with my mother. My dad had a friend up in the front seat with him. We, of course, were not restrained in seatbelts, so as a result, we were bouncing around and playing like six children would. Suddenly, someone accidentally opened the door, and out fell Tom. Although my mother knew he had fallen out, she was so shocked that when she tried to scream, no sound came from her mouth. We said nothing. As a matter of fact, we probably just continued to bounce around and have fun. A car pulled up next to my father, honking his horn and screaming until my dad pulled over. By that time, we were all screaming as well. My father turned the car around, and we went back to retrieve Tom. Miraculously, he had suffered only scrapes, bruises, and a broken collarbone.

My mother was pretty amazing, considering she had eight children, three of whom were in diapers at one time. She probably did not know what a good night of sleep felt like for years. Anyway, on one particular occasion, she was just beginning to relax after a hard day's work. We were all snug in our beds at the time. The boys were in the upstairs bedroom, and Maureen, Margie, and I were in the bedroom across the hall from Mom and Dad. I can picture my mom sitting in the living room, smoking her cigarette, enjoying the quiet. Her relaxation was disturbed by the phone ringing. When she answered, it was Mrs. Zerio, who lived across the street, informing my mother that the boys were not in their beds. Instead, they had chosen to take a trip out on the roof of the house. All four of them were neatly lined up on the top of the roof, surveying the neighborhood. My mother's response? In her heavy Irish accent, she commented to Mrs. Zerio, "Ah, well, they'll come in when they get good and tired." She sat back down and continued to enjoy her cigarette and quiet time.

My parents were great Catholics, but it was my mother who firmly believed in all the great traditions and practices of the Catholic Church. She also had a few of her own traditions, in particular, our stormy weather tradition. As I look back on it now, she must have been very frightened of storms, and especially tornado warnings. It seemed like whenever the skies turned dark, she'd break out the candles, light them, and we'd all fall to our knees in prayer. I can still picture us, kneeling in a circle around lighted candles, saying our "Hail Marys" in hopes that we wouldn't die. Keep in mind, this was shortly after I had seen *The Wizard of Oz* for the first time. I was convinced for many years that surely, during one storm or another, our house was going to take flight and land in some Godforsaken place.

My mom had two "shrines" in our house. At first, it was just a picture of the Sacred Heart with a candle underneath it. However, years later, John F. Kennedy got his own little shrine, right next to Jesus Christ, lighted and everything. In her eyes, he was as close to Jesus as one could come. She was so proud that we had an Irish Catholic in the White House.

We had another great tradition in our family which occurred during the Christmas season. We were raised to believe that this was more a "giving" than a "receiving" time. So, most of my siblings and I would bundle ourselves up a few days before Christmas and go Christmas caroling in the neighborhood. Most of our neighbors knew us, so they would generously reward us for our singing. After we had raised a reasonable amount of money, we would go home and prepare for our shopping trip. This was where my dad entered the picture. My mother didn't drive until she was in her seventies, so my dad had to shuttle us around. The problem was that my dad was not a patient shopper. He hated shopping. So, after we had raised our Christmas money, he would drive us to the mall, drop us off at the front of the store, and tell us we had an hour to buy what we needed. I can still picture us leaping out of the car, tearing into the store, and purchasing whatever cheap presents we could get our hands on. It made for great memories, though, and lots of fun.

Another story involved my eldest brother, Ed. When he was in first grade he came home one day after school and announced that he was going to be in a talent show. My mother was amused in a motherly sort of way and asked Ed exactly what he planned to do in the talent show. Ed replied that he was going to sing. When my mother realized that he was serious she asked, "What are you going to sing? You don't know any songs." Ed very insistently replied that he was going to sing 'White Christmas, just like Bing Crosby". Time passed and my mother pretty much forgot about the talent show. Before the event, Ed reminded my parents and they were surprised to hear that he was still in the talent show. Anyway, the night of the event, they filed into the auditorium and took a seat. When it was Ed's turn to perform, my mom and dad heard the woman behind them nudge her husband and say, "Wait until you hear this little guy sing". Ed opened his mouth, began to sing and my mother's jaw dropped to the floor. Thus, my brother's singing career was launched.

The house that my dad built in Centerline, Michigan, outside of Detroit in the late 1940s, was considered to be located in the country at the time. It soon became a suburb. By the time I was born, it was a cozy neighborhood, still a great place to raise a family. We had great cultural diversity on the block. We were closest to the Zerios, an immigrant Italian family. When we didn't want to be Irish anymore, we just took a trip across the street, and we were immediately immersed in another culture. It was great to go to their house and listen to them speak Italian, even greater to enjoy their many Italian dishes that they were so willing to share with us. They lost their father very early to a heart attack. He was only in his late forties. Their mother did a tremendous job of holding them together. She worked very hard at Krogers. She certainly demonstrated the concept of a struggling single mother. She had seven children, the majority still less than eighteen years of age. She simply did what she had to do, very willingly. In addition to mothering her own family, she was a second mother to all of us. Their house was very "colorful." Mrs. Zerio's method of discipline was to scream in Italian and grasp whatever was close and send it flying through the air. Most often, she'd take the time to remove her shoe, and then everyone knew it was time to duck! It's quite humorous as I look back on it now. She was a great lady, and we all loved her dearly.

Most of the kids on our street attended St. Clement's, the neighborhood Catholic school. I have pleasant memories of the experience. The

Dominican sisters were very loving and caring to me. Sure, they had their idiosyncrasies, but that is true of the general population. I vividly remember one day in second grade, when the sister called me out into the hall. I thought I must have done something wrong. Instead, she had purchased a beautiful white blouse for me and didn't want to give it to me in front of the class. I was so touched. My blouse must have looked pretty worn. Most likely, this happened during one of the times when Dad had been laid off at Chrysler, or maybe after the fire we had one year around Christmas time.

Growing up in a family of seven children with a blue-collar working father meant that there was never an abundance of money. But I never felt poor. I always felt safe and secure, and both of my parents worked extremely hard to provide for us. As we each entered school, there really wasn't enough money to send us to a Catholic school. My parents, however, made it a priority. In one of my mother's favorite sayings, "Where there's a will, there's a way," they found the way. My mom would walk to work every day and begin her shift as the cafeteria cook at the high school. I'm sure this was a big sacrifice, because although she was a wonderful cook, she never particularly enjoyed it. But, a Catholic education we would have!

Speaking of money shortages, on many occasions, when Chrysler was cutting back, we received welfare food. I distinctly remember the canned dried eggs and the canned meat in the silver metal cans. It was far from delicious, but we ate it anyway. There were a few Christmases that revolved around a knock on the door. The Goodfellows would be standing there with baskets of food and presents for all of us.

In addition, to help subsidize my father's income, someone (I presume it was my mother) got the brilliant idea that we could pick cherries for a few weeks during the summer. Of course, most of the people picking cherries were Mexican migrant workers. A white, Irish family was a real rarity. Anyway, we'd hop in the car and head all the way up to the

Mission Peninsula, which was north of Traverse City, Michigan. Back then, it was a full day's journey. When we arrived, we would unpack the car and move into a tent, which would be our home for two or three weeks. Dad would pick cherries on the weekend, then go back home to work his regular week at Chrysler and return again on the weekend. I can still remember how it felt to strap on the bucket to the front of me with the metal hooks on each side. Then we'd pick cherries like crazy, unload them into wooden boxes on the ground, and begin picking again. I was never allowed to go too high on the ladders because I was too young.

I think we picked cherries for two or three summers. Eventually, we graduated to cabin status. Our cherry-picking days ended on a sour note. Apparently, during the middle of the night, a family got into a violent domestic dispute. The police and ambulance were called, and a big scene erupted. Everyone woke up, and there was a lot of shouting and screaming. I never really found out exactly what happened, but we never went back to pick cherries again.

During a few other summers, when money was scarce, I attended Camp Stapleton and my brothers went to Camp Ozinham. I guess they were camps for low-income families, although I never realized that fact until much later. I don't remember where they were located in Michigan, but I do remember that we had lots of fun there.

I loved having four brothers. I grew up a tomboy and figured I could do almost anything they could do. They taught me how to play many sports, including basketball and baseball. As kids, during the summer, we would listen to the Tigers, walk down to the end of the block with a bunch of neighborhood kids, and play baseball in an empty lot—and ice skate at the same place in the winter. I played softball with a group of girls in grade school from the time we were eight or nine. When we were freshman in high school, all of us made the varsity softball team, which was pretty unusual. My brothers taught me all about sports and "boy" things, but my sisters, in every sense, were my "soul sisters." We could communicate with each other without speaking. When we were small, the three of us slept in the same double bed. Later, when we moved upstairs and had two double beds, we would fight about who had to sleep alone ... not who would have a bed all to themselves. Maureen was my hero, my mentor, my model in life. I had a tremendous amount of respect for her, and I tried to emulate everything she did. She was three years older and wiser, and gently guided me through childhood, adolescence, and beyond. Margie, my younger sister, is four years younger than I. I loved being the sister in the middle. I could learn from Maureen and pass those same lessons on to Margie. I had the best of both worlds. I distinctly remember the image of the three of us on many occasions locking our arms together, kicking up our heels, and singing, "Sisters, sisters, there were never more devoted sisters." In many ways, we were each other's best friend.

Changes

A fter my sophomore year in high school, my father retired, and my parents decided to move to a small town in northern Michigan called Harrison. I was sixteen, Tom was seventeen, and Margie was twelve. Needless to say, none of us wanted to move and live far from our friends and neighbors. All of my other siblings, including Maureen, would stay in Centerline and work.

There were many visits by my older brothers and sister, but it was still a lonely time for me. It was not easy to make new friends because I left behind the things I loved: my friends and my sports teams from Centerline. Harrison did not have sports programs for girls. As a result, I spent lots of time studying, working to save money for college, and hanging out with my one good friend, Debbie.

In addition to my friendship with Debbie, my short stint in Harrison gave me the opportunity to meet a young man named Mark Graham. When people ask how we met, the truthful answer is "in a truck stop," called Snow Snake Service. He pumped gas, and I waited on tables in the restaurant. It was a different world from the sheltered Catholic community I had just left. I quickly learned the "way of the world" in the truck stop, turned down many distasteful proposals, and decided that I had to make a better life for myself.

During that summer of 1967, Maureen came up north for a visit driving a brand-new red convertible, a Plymouth Barracuda. It was *so cool!* I can remember cruising around town, thinking that I would do the same thing and buy a super-fine car when I graduated from high school. I also remember that I thought she had completely lost her mind when she sold the Barracuda a few months later and announced that she was going to college. So, when I was a junior in high school, Maureen started college.

Although our family was now in two or three different locations in the state, we still managed to have family holidays together. Everyone would drive up to Harrison at Thanksgiving, Christmas, and Easter. Maureen visited often to tell tales of college life. Gradually, I gave up the dream of buying a new, fancy car and thought that I, too, might go to college. Maureen helped me fill out college entrance applications, sign up for the A.C.T. tests, and apply for loans and grants. I was ecstatic when I was accepted at Central Michigan University in Mount Pleasant. Even though it was only thirty miles from home, it felt far enough away.

Life was new and different for Maureen, too. She had chosen Eastern Michigan University as her institution of higher learning. She was entering her junior year when I graduated from high school. She had become active in student government with two fellow students, Dennis Hertel and Milton Mack, with whom she would remain lifelong friends. She eventually worked for Dennis and was his "right-hand man" when he became a member of the Michigan House of Representatives. She later followed him when he became a U.S. Congressman. Milton remained in Michigan and became a probate court judge in Detroit, Michigan. Maureen dated Milt on and off for many years, but they never became serious enough to marry.

In addition to Milt, Maureen dated a few other men for whom she cared deeply. The man that won her heart, however, was Richard DeShetler. Dick had been previously married and had three children, which might have frightened off other women, but not Maureen. She fell in love with him, and there was no looking back. When they married, his children, Scott, Jeri, and Jill, became her stepchildren. Initially, the children harbored a natural resentment, undoubtedly feeling that Maureen was trying to take the place of their mother. Over the years, however, it was wonderful to observe the special bond that developed between Maureen and Scott, Jeri, and Jill. Genuine love replaced the earlier resentment.

I continued to date my "truck stop" man through my four years of college at Central Michigan. He had decided to attend Northern Michigan University in Marquette, so we were not able to see each other very often. We wrote to each other, and our romance developed through our letters and the time we spent together during the summer. I received a letter from Mark almost every day. After he finished studying, he would write to me before he went to bed. I, on the other hand, would fall asleep many nights before I got a letter off to him.

Attending separate colleges was probably a good thing for us. We couldn't be distracted by one another, and it allowed us to concentrate on our schoolwork. However, when it came time for student teaching in our senior year, we made plans to get closer to one another geographically. The plan was that I would try to get a teaching assignment in the northern part of the Lower Peninsula and Mark would try to get an assignment in the lower Upper Peninsula. Our plans didn't work out very well. We found out just before Christmas break in 1972 that Mark's assignment would be in Green Bay, Wisconsin! My assignment ended up close to home, approximately fifteen miles from Harrison, in Gladwin, Michigan. The writing was on the wall. If we were lucky, we might be able to see each other once or twice from January to May, as 1973 rolled in.

As fate would have it, it just so happened that Mark's beloved car, his 1964 Falcon Flyer, decided to blow up in March. He had to have a car to get to school each day. His younger brother, Kenny, came to the rescue. Kenny was talented with car repairs and engines, so he had an extra car, a Camaro, which Mark could use while he finished his student teaching assignment. The problem was that we had to get the car to Mark. Arrangements were made for the car to be transported by ferry across Lake Michigan. Mark would board the ferry in Wisconsin on a Friday, spend the weekend, pick up the car, drive to Ludington, Michigan, to board the ferry with the car, and return to Green Bay. It just so happened that all of this was to happen over St. Patrick's Day weekend. So, his parents and I traveled to Ludington on that Friday to pick Mark up. It had been snowing during the morning, and there was some accumulation of snow on the ground. As we traveled toward Ludington, the snow and the wind picked up considerably. When we arrived in Ludington that evening, we were told that the ferry had not been able to leave Wisconsin due to the storm, and it would probably leave in the morning. Great! Rather than driving home in the storm, we made reservations at a hotel in Ludington with the hopes of seeing Mark in the morning.

When I awoke the following morning, things did not look good. In fact, they looked worse. The wind was still blowing, and there was probably a foot of snow outside. We went to the docks to check on the ferry and were told that the ship had not left during the night and was actually still docked in Wisconsin. Consequently, it turns out the ship did not leave Wisconsin until very early Sunday morning. It arrived in Ludington at approximately ten a.m. and would return to Wisconsin at eleven. We were able to have breakfast together, but Mark had to turn around and re-board the same ship with the car that Kenny had driven to Ludington that morning. Needless to say, it was agonizing. With love and hormones raging, we hugged and kissed hello and goodbye within an hour .

The remaining months apart seemed like eternity. Finally, we both successfully completed our student teaching, and summer gloriously appeared. It wasn't long, however, before our lives would go in separate directions again.

Families of Our Own

When I graduated from college in 1973, I was hired by a school district in Midland, Michigan, to teach high school English. Mark decided to attend graduate school at Michigan State University. We had begun talking about marriage, but I was thousands of dollars in debt and didn't feel like I could comfortably marry until I had paid off some of my college debts. I taught in Midland for three years before marriage became a reality.

I was the first of the girls to marry. I married Mark in November of 1976. Mark had finished graduate school in urban planning and had accepted a job as a city planner in Delta Township, which was a suburb of Lansing, Michigan. I was able to get another teaching job in a small town, Morrice, just east of Lansing.

Maureen and Dick were married the next May, in 1977. They had a great marriage, and had transformed the 1890s house they had purchased into a beautiful home. Renovating the house for Dick, a General Motors engineer, was no problem. We often gathered there for Christmas, Dick's famous barbeques, or for no reason at all. Scott, Jeri, and Jill were there often, and they became a part of our family. It wasn't until ten years later, when Dick was getting ready for retirement that "family" took on a new definition for Maureen and Dick. I remember it as if it were yesterday.

We were gathered at Maureen and Dick's on a winter day in 1987 when Maureen called me upstairs. I sat on the bed, and she asked me not to tell anyone the surprising news that she was pregnant. This news was just too good to keep secret. I went screaming down the stairs and announced it to everyone. Maureen and Dick were not angry. They just laughed and made the comment that they no longer needed to struggle with the issue of how to tell everyone. Maureen was almost forty years old, and Dick was close to fifty. So much for any thoughts of retirement! Dick might have been able to retire from General Motors, but his life would continue to be busy in a very different way.

His new job, and his new joy, came nine months later. She was named Megan ... and she didn't come easily. Margie and I had left our jobs on Thursday afternoon, October 7, 1987, proclaiming that we would be back the next day with news of a new niece. Our job, as labor coaches, was to help Maureen through the delivery process and give Dick breaks whenever he needed a breather. Maureen's labor continued through the next day, but she could not push Megan out. A c-section was performed on the evening of the eighth of October. Megan was a healthy, beautiful little girl with a big head, just like her father. It was no wonder Maureen could not push her out.

Megan was a great baby. Margie and I were the godmothers, and Mark was her godfather. We visited Maureen, Dick, and Megan as often as we could, and we took many trips together. Megan was the type of baby that loved to go wherever you were going. When she was an infant, I can recall Dick holding her like a football at his side, with Megan facing out. She always wanted to see what everyone was doing. As she grew, she never wanted to go to bed, and the bedtime ritual and snack could go on for an hour or so. She loved to be where the action was as a child and remains that way today.

Remarkably, eleven months after Megan was born, Mark and I were blessed with a baby boy. We were "blessed" in every sense of the word.

Mark and I had tried to conceive a child for many years. We had lots of fun trying, but it never happened. We had undergone the rigors of infertility treatments. Both of us had surgical procedures done, which, it turns out, were not the reason for our infertility. We tried everything but in vitro fertilization. We both figured it was very expensive and not guaranteed to work. As fate would have it, we had filed for adoption with Lansing Catholic Social Services on St. Patricks Day in 1980. We had become tired of the doctor's appointments, the prodding and poking. We surrendered our problem to God and put this problem in His hands. Don't get me wrong—we had our questions. Why was this happening? Wouldn't we make great parents? We could look around and see multitudes of children being raised by questionable parents.

We waited many long years for the much-anticipated call from the adoption agency. It finally came in early September of 1988. The agency was ready to begin the final stage of the adoption process, which normally takes about a year. They begin the process with an initial interview, do some home studies, more interviews, and in nine months or so, assuming we were acceptable candidates, we would have a baby!

We were called for our first interview on a Friday in late September. It was a tough interview. We were asked all kinds of hypothetical questions such as, "What will you do when your child is two years old and has a tantrum in a grocery store? What will you do when your child is sixteen and you find drugs in his/her bedroom?" We really hadn't considered such things. We just wanted a baby. We answered the questions the best we could and left wondering if our responses were "parent worthy."

The very next Monday, Mark got a call from the adoption agency. They wanted to know if we could meet with them again that day after work. We were sure that we had "flunked" the initial interview and this would be the end of our dreams. We were shocked when we sat down and the social worker said, "I think we might have a baby for you." Apparently, a child had been born here, in Lansing, and he seemed to "fit" our family. The birth parents had requested a non-smoking, religious family. We had stated on our application that we would lovingly accept a bi-racial child, and the baby was Hispanic-American. The birth parents were struggling with the decision of releasing him for adoption, and they had thirty days to make up their minds. In the meantime, the year-long adoption process would be shortened to thirty days!

After the meeting with the social worker, I literally ran to church. I was filled with such a tremendous sense of joy and thanksgiving. While I was in the church, I heard our choir director, William, practicing upstairs, so I ran up to tell him the good news. We talked for a long time, and he shared in my obvious excitement.

There are significant moments in our lives which we never forget. As a child of the sixties, we experienced many, including the assassination of President Kennedy. I remember where I was, what the weather was like, etc. The same holds true for the morning of November 29, 1988 when Mark and I traveled to Saint Vincent Home. I remember the way the room looked and smelled and how the sun was peeking through the shades. I remember how we waited for the door to open. Finally, it did, and in walked Matthew's foster mother, holding him in her arms. I cried when she gave him to me. It was just so incredibly joyful, and he was so beautiful. He was thirty-seven days old. We named him "Matthew," which means "gift of God."

Matthew, like Megan, was a great baby. Megan was thrilled with her new playmate. Maureen and I would get together often, and she was a great source of information for me. Megan had just reached the growth and development milestone markers that Matthew would be entering.

As Matthew and Megan grew, our trips and outings became more frequent. We would shop, go to the zoo, visit parks, and take trips to Florida together to see Grandma and Grandpa. In addition, we would take winter and summer vacations together. I remember one summer when our entire extended family rented a cottage in Omena, a small town in northern Michigan. On a visit to a quaint town nearby, Mark, Dick, Megan, and Matt played in a park while "the girls" were "set free" to go shopping. Maureen and Margie decided to shop on one side of the street, while I scoped out the shops on the opposite side of the street. While I was browsing the shops, I discovered this great lipstick that went on clear, but would turn the color of your mood, sort of like the old mood rings. I snatched up the bargain, paid the money, and quickly applied it with no mirror. I went back to the park and checked on the kids and talked with Dick and Mark for a few minutes.

Eventually, I resumed my shopping and tried to locate my sisters. It wasn't long before I spotted them down the street. As I got closer, I could see them staring at me with a perplexed look on their faces. When we finally reached each other, they immediately wanted to know what I had been eating. I told them I had eaten nothing. Then they asked what had happened to my lips, because they were the brightest, hottest pink they had ever seen, and looked quite ridiculous. I explained that I had purchased this "special" lipstick, grabbed a mirror, and checked myself out. They were absolutely correct in their evaluation of my prized purchase. I told them that I had stopped and talked to both Dick and Mark, wearing my special lipstick, and they had said nothing. They found my comment even more amusing than my lipstick. Did I really expect that these two men would notice that my lips were the color of a flamingo? It was just so typical and one of the humorous memories that we shared.

On July 17, 1990, we celebrated my mother's eightieth birthday at Maureen and Dick's house with all of the family, some cousins, and the Zerios. Matthew was almost two, and Megan was almost three. Megan used whatever occasion she could to let Matthew know that she was older and, for the time being, bigger. We were all gathered around my mother as we sang "Happy Birthday" to her. I remember Matthew and Megan standing in front of the kiddie pool as we sang. Near the end of the song, I could see Megan looking at Matt with a wee bit of mischief in her eyes. As soon as we finished singing, she turned to Matthew, gave him a pretty good push, and down he went in the water. Being the good sport that he was, he just popped up and pronounced, "Oh, my goodness!"

Later, as they grew, their conversations and play became more sophisticated. On another visit to Maureen's house, I observed the kids in a different situation. Maureen and Dick had a big wrap-around porch on their house. We had made the kids a picnic lunch, and they were sitting at their kiddie table around the corner from me, enjoying their lunch together. They were just talking, like a typical four- and five-year-old, when Matthew asked Megan, "Hey, Megan, do you know what 'bewilder' means?"

Megan thought about the question for a minute and replied, "No, what does it mean?"

Matthew said, "Hurt, bewilder means hurt."

I have no idea where Matthew came up with that, but anyway, Megan was really quiet for a minute, and then she said, "You know, Matthew, I have a lot of bewilders. I have one here, and here, and here," as she proceeded to point out little scrapes and bruises that she had on her arms and legs. They were always so cute together.

We continued to have many joyous family gatherings during the first few years of Megan's and Matt's early childhood. For me, I had experienced almost forty years of a "charmed" existence. We often commented that our parents, who had so bravely left Ireland so many years ago, had created a great legacy. They birthed eight children and raised seven. At this point, they had over fifteen grandchildren. None of us had ever been in trouble with the law, and most of us had college degrees. We are successful because of them. They placed great importance on three things: providing us with a good education, something they never received; loving and caring for each other; and most importantly, centering our lives around the church and faith in God. These ideological beliefs were the basis for countless family discussions.

We didn't know then, and would not know until many years later, how much we would rely on these important lessons that our parents so firmly established in our minds and hearts.

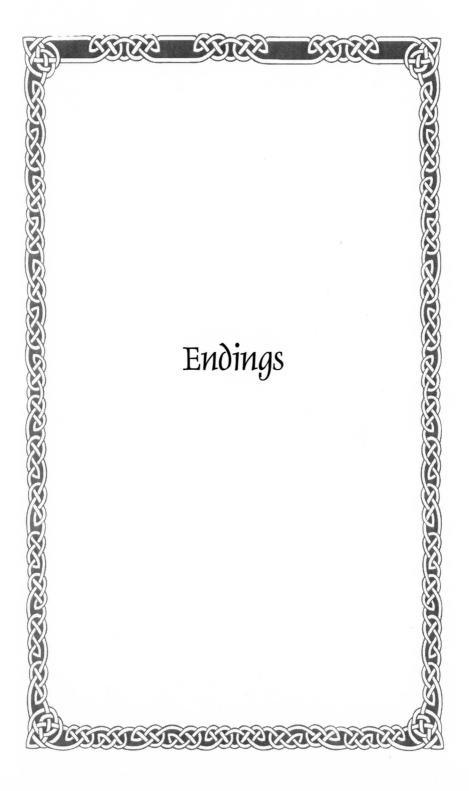

Endings

Dad

On a cold day in January of 1992, I came home from work to find a message on our recorder from my mother. She stated that an ambulance had taken Dad to the hospital, and that he had suffered a minor stroke. I called her that night, and she said he was doing well. He was eating, but could not talk. I went to bed relieved and hopeful. He had just celebrated his ninety-fourth birthday a few weeks earlier on December 10th. He was a "young-looking" ninety-four-year-old man. In fact, he was still bowling every Monday with my mom and neighborhood friends. He still went to dances. My brother, Pat, and his family had just visited Florida that Christmas, and he and Dad had gone for a long walk together. People marveled that Dad was on no medication. When he had his physical at age ninety, the doctor was very interested in his lifestyle. He wanted to know what he ate, what he did for exercise, and basically his life history. We were all convinced he would live to be a hundred. In fact, he laughed many times about the ninetieth birthday card that I sent him. I enclosed ninety dollars for him and told him that I couldn't wait to make it one hundred dollars.

For all these reasons, I found it difficult to believe that he had suffered a stroke. The next day, I got a call from Mom that made me shudder. She said that it turned out that the little bits of food that my father had eaten the day before had not traveled down to his stomach. He had lost his ability to swallow as a result of the stroke. His condition was much more serious than we had initially thought.

I was talking to family members in no time. Maureen's most recent position with Representative Dennis Hertel had ended in January, so she was available to make a trip. Dick was somewhat retired at the time. I was teaching in a small town south of Lansing, Eaton Rapids, but had accumulated many sick days that I could use for family illnesses. It didn't take us long to decide that we needed to go to Florida. We got into my van, and Dick drove almost non-stop to Florida. He rested for a few hours while Maureen and I took turns driving.

We went immediately to the hospital in Ocala. I wasn't prepared to see my dad as he was. He looked tired, and the stroke had distorted his face. It was obvious that he recognized us. His frustration at not being able to speak was also very obvious.

The doctors were not optimistic and suggested a nursing home. My siblings and I had discussed that option previously, but we vowed that a nursing home would not be where our dear parents would spend the remaining days of their lives. The doctors convinced us, however, that Dad needed physical therapy and that the nursing home would be the best place to get the rehabilitation he needed. We reluctantly admitted him to a nursing home in Ocala, which was about twenty miles from their home.

Initially, he did very well. My mother and brothers were pleased with his progress. They stated he was to the point where he was walking the full length of the hall holding onto my mother's hand. We had been taking turns going down to Florida to help with his care and visit the nursing home on a regular basis. On the day my brothers left, they stopped at the desk and discussed my father's feisty personality. He was a very proud man. They knew he would try to get up when he wanted to go to the bathroom. A few days after they left, he was buzzing the night help for assistance, and when they didn't come, he tried to get out of bed by himself. He fell down, struck his head, and was knocked unconscious. We speculate that he suffered another stroke at that time, because he was never able to regain the progress he had made. He never walked again. A short time later, he developed pneumonia which became critical. En route to the hospital, he apparently suffered a heart attack and was put on life support, against his wishes.

His prognosis was not good at all. We were all notified by Mom, and within a very short time, more than twenty of us, children and grandchildren, were on our way to Florida. Upon our arrival, we were once again, greeted by a nightmarish scene. He was hooked up to every kind of imaginable support machine, and only a few of us could be in the room with him at a given time. Finally, Mom was called into a room by the doctor, with the immediate family present. We had to decide whether to continue the life support or let nature take its course. The doctors were convinced he would last only a few hours after being pulled from life support. The machines ware turned off, and we waited for God to take him home.

Instead, the following morning he opened his blue, Irish, still-twinkling eyes. Pat looked at him and said, "Hey Pop, you're supposed to be dead!" We all laughed and breathed a huge sigh of relief. My Mom had always joked, "You can't kill a bad thing" in reference to my Dad's longevity. We were all so happy that he had decided to spend some more time with us. The doctors just shook their heads in amazement and probably wished all of us would clear out of the hospital. In reality, they commented that it was obvious that he had some more living to do with his amazing family.

We took Dad home a few days later. We all felt we could take care of him at home, where he belonged. We regretted we had not taken him home immediately after the stroke. We learned how to suction his throat to keep the fluids from entering his lungs. We were also taught how to tube-feed him, because he never regained his ability to swallow. We set up a schedule to take turns helping with his care. In addition, we hired a neighbor to help, and visiting nurses came a few times each week. Our biggest help came from my nephew, Corey. He was in the Air Force and was discharged a few months early so he could help care for his grandpa. He moved in with Mom and Dad and worked as a caregiver while attending college.

I was able to visit three or four more times before Dad died. I fondly remember that I was with him on Father's Day. I took Dad for a few strolls in his wheelchair, and it was great to get him outside in the fresh air. Although he couldn't communicate with me, I knew by his hand gestures what he would have said had he been able to talk. Dad loved the outdoors and would always make remarks about the flowers, or the trees, or the canal in his backyard.

I also took him to church on Father's Day. In spite of admonitions not to attempt such an outing, I was determined. I knew it was possible, for I had internalized my mother's favorite saying, "Where there's a will, there's a way!" My feeling was that he could literally rot in the bed, or we could attempt to give his remaining days some quality. It took the good part of the morning to get him ready. He was able to shave most of his face. Getting him dressed was another matter. It took three of us to accomplish that feat, and three of us to load him into the car. Sliding him out of the car and into the wheelchair went smoothly when we arrived at the church. It was just wonderful to have him in the church he had attended one or two times per week since moving to Florida. When Mass was over, getting him back in the car was nearly disastrous. He got stuck with half of his body on the seat of the car and the other half falling out of the wheelchair. Thank goodness for the kind woman in the parking lot who asked if she could assist with what appeared to be a very difficult task. With an extra pair of hands, we were able to boost him in the seat. We returned home safe and sound.

We took turns visiting during the summer. In spite of our attempts to prevent them, Dad got some nasty bed sores on his heels and hip. Still, he was able to live at home for six months, surrounded by people who loved him. On September 5, 1992, Dad died with my mom at his side. Maureen, Margie, and I flew to Florida for the funeral. This was my first experience with the death of a family member, and I cried most of the way on the plane. It was hard for me to believe that my father was really gone.

This time, only Dad's immediate children flew down for the funeral. The grandchildren stayed in Michigan. There were many events at the funeral that were so typically "Dad" and gave us a feeling that he would always be with us. Even the weather cooperated in a McGlinchey sort of way. Yet another of my mother's favorite sayings, "Happy is the bride that the sun shines on, happy is the corpse that the rain rains on" gave us all a reason for reflection. The day was beautifully sunny up to the point when the hearse arrived at the church. As the driver got out to open the back of the hearse, it started pouring rain. It continued to rain until we arrived at the gravesite with Dad. As we began to leave the cemetery, the clouds broke open and the sun reappeared.

Another event during the funeral confirmed that Dad was still with us, but in a different way. My mom had an "angel" friend, who sat with her countless hours while Dad was sick in the hospital and at home. Her name was Joanne, and she drove a beautiful Lincoln Continental at the time. It was arranged that Mom would ride with her from the church to the gravesite after the church ceremony. As we began to leave the church, Joanne got to her car and realized that she had locked her keys in the car. Another good friend of my Mom's, named Anne, volunteered to drive family members to the gravesite. The make of her car? It was none other than a beautiful Chrysler, the company that my dad had worked for most of his life. It was as if he were saying, "As you say goodbye, travel in a car made by the company I worked for all those years."

A few days later, as Maureen, Margie, Mom, and I were leaving Florida and heading to the airport to return to Michigan, we got in the car and turned on the radio. The song my brother sang at Dad's funeral entitled, "Morning Has Broken," was playing. We all just looked at each other, assured that he was with us in spirit.

After my dad died, I was worried about my mother. I thought she might just decide to die herself without him. She commented many times how much she missed him, but she continued to go to Florida by herself, live by herself, and enjoy her friends in Florida for many more years. I shouldn't have doubted her strength. The lessons of the past should have been enough to tell me that anyone who could get on a ship at nineteen and leave her family and home was, indeed, a pillar of strength.

I forgot to mention that as we were sitting around the house after the funeral, the women in the family decided we should do something "fun" in Dad's memory. I don't remember who suggested it, but someone came up with the idea to go to Las Vegas. We all agreed that it sounded like a good idea, but most likely would never happen. We were wrong. In February, all the women, plus some friends of friends, boarded a plane in various locations for a four-day weekend in Dad's honor. There were probably twenty or more of us booked into the same hotel. None of us cared much for gambling, but we went to sightsee, enjoy the weather, watch some great entertainment, and play a few slot machines. We had a great time, and I'm sure Dad liked the fact that we were all together, having fun in his memory.

My dad had a great life. He lived to the ripe old age of ninety-four. Certainly the suffering he endured at the end of his life was difficult for him and for us. However, his death was understandable. It was an example of the natural cycle of life. Nothing, however, could help me to understand or prepare for what would transpire during the next few years of my life.

Dick

Life returned to normal. At the end of March in 1993, Mark, Maureen, Megan, Matthew, and I drove down to Florida to visit Mom. We vacationed in the sun with the kids, went to Disney World, and enjoyed our time with "Grandma." Dick had stayed at home because he was working part-time as an engineer in "retirement" and, at the same time, was remodeling their upstairs bathroom. He planned to have it finished when we returned a week later.

On our drive back to Michigan, Maureen touched base with Dick two or three times. He reported that "everything was good at home with the exception of the bathroom remodeling job." He had punctured the water pipes twice as he was rerouting the plumbing, and things were not going back together very well. He seemed frustrated and confused. I remember Maureen commenting that Dick never seemed confused about such things.

In early May, Maureen called, and I immediately sensed that something was wrong. She had been to the doctor with Dick, and the news was not good. A brain tumor was the suspected cause of the confusion and headaches. He would be going to the hospital the following week for a stereotactic brain biopsy. The doctors would remove brain tissue to determine if the tumor was malignant.

I met Maureen at the hospital. We sat in the surgical waiting room with Dick's daughter, Jeri, her fiancée, Chris, and Chris' mother. Jeri and Chris were planning a wedding in July and were discussing whether or not to postpone the wedding. Jeri was a nurse and worked at the hospital where the biopsy was being performed. All the preliminary tests indicated very serious problems, and I think Jeri and Chris were preparing themselves for the worst because they knew more than we did.

We saw Dick later that day, and he was obviously uncomfortable. He stated he could probably withstand anything, but he would not let them "drill holes" in his head again. All we could do now was wait and pray. Dick's life totally changed during this time period. From the moment the doctors were suspicious that something was seriously wrong, Dick's life, as he knew it, was gone. He could no longer drive, work, participate in strenuous exercise, hunt, sail, or do any of the activities he loved. The chance of suffering a seizure, and risking grave injury, was just too great.

In early May, our worst suspicions were confirmed. Dick had a brain tumor, a *glioblastoma multiforme* (both sides of his brain). The prognosis: very grim. It was recommended he get his affairs in order, and death would most likely occur in three to six months. We all reacted in the same way, utter shock and disbelief. He appeared to be so healthy.

There weren't many treatment options for this type of brain tumor. Dick could decide to seek treatment, which in most cases prolonged life somewhat, or withhold treatment and attempt to enjoy his remaining time on this earth. He decided to do the treatment option. I'm sure that he decided to do this for Maureen and his children, and especially for his pride and joy, Megan.

Fortunately, as of January, 1993, Maureen was still not employed for the first time in twenty years because her friend and boss, Dennis, had decided not to run again for legislative office in 1992. She worried about her unemployment, but I assured her that when the time came, she would have no trouble finding a job. It seemed that wherever we went, people knew her. You could not go to well-known Detroit establishments such as Tiger Stadium or the Fox Theater without being approached by someone with hugs and well-wishes for her. We often suggested that if she ran for office, she would surely be elected.

When Maureen's job ended that January, the plan was for her to take a few months off, enjoy Megan's kindergarten year at school, volunteer often, and just relax. Things took a very different turn with Dick's diagnosis. Yes, it was fortunate that she was not working outside her home during that time. But it was so unfortunate what the next few months would hold for her and the rest of her family. There was nothing we could do to kill this monster that had settled in Dick's brain. We felt helpless.

We were all there as Dick made the many trips for radiation and chemotherapy treatments. Usually, Jeri and Dick's brother, Dave, transported him to and from the hospital. We (Maureen's siblings) traveled on the weekends and sometimes during the week to lend a hand with laundry, cooking, yard work, and other chores that needed to be done.

Over Memorial Day weekend, my sister Margie and her husband Peter, who is a builder, held a "house-raising party" near Kalamazoo. About thirty of us were there to help them get the house "off the ground." The foundation had been poured, and the floor joists for the first floor had been installed when most of us arrived. It was amazing how much more was done when Maureen and Dick arrived on Saturday afternoon. We were all so glad to see them. We ran to the car to greet them. Dick looked much better, but it was painful for all of us to watch him. Normally, his engineering skills would have propelled him into action. He'd have a hammer in his hand in no time, and he'd be swinging away. Not this day, and not ever again.

Dick was the perfect spouse for Maureen. For instance, he was extremely patient. Maureen had hundreds of positive character traits, but punctuality was not one of them, and Dick understood that trying to hurry her made no difference. Dick, like Maureen, was fun-loving and very social. He had work friends, neighborhood friends, Upper Peninsula friends, and sailing friends. Sailing was his passion. As a matter of fact, he and Maureen first met on the docks before the annual Port Huron to Mackinaw race in the mid 1970s. He also sailed in the Chicago to Mackinaw race many a time. He loved the water, and the beauty and thrill of sailing.

Two or three weeks after Memorial Day, Maureen and Dick's very close friends, Roger and Callie, had a support party for Dick. Family and many friends of Dick and Maureen's gathered in Pontiac, Michigan, in a gesture of good will and in an effort to send all of our positive energy Dick's way. He was in good spirits that day, even though he was well into his treatment regimen. He was taking large doses of steroids, which were beginning to give him a "puffy" appearance. We celebrated Dick for being such a great man, and when it was time for me to leave, being the gentleman that he was, he walked me to my car and thanked me for everything. We exchanged "I love you's," and he closed my door. As I drove away, I could see him in my rear-view mirror, waving goodbye. That image of him with the sun setting behind his back has vividly remained in my mind.

On June 26, 1993, Jeri and Chris were married. Everyone attempted to set aside their sadness to celebrate with Jeri and Chris, and all was going well until the "daddy/daughter" dance. Dick and Jeri danced to the song "Unforgettable," and through the entire dance, there wasn't a dry eye in the room. It had been two months since Dick's diagnosis, and already he was beginning to have trouble with his balance. After the dance, Maureen became very emotional, so we took a walk around the parking lot. She couldn't stop crying and expressing what everyone felt

... what a terrible nightmare we were living, and how she just wanted it to stop.

As mentioned earlier, as an extended family, we had taken many summer vacations together, and Maureen was usually the "great planner." She would find a huge cottage up north near Sutton's Bay, where her friends Sharon and Wayne lived, call all of her siblings, and we'd all spend a week together. We shared many great moments gazing out on Sutton's Bay around a campfire. We would visit the sand dunes; go golfing, bike ride, swim, and shop. Each "family" would take turns cooking and preparing the meals for the day.

After Jeri and Chris' wedding, we had planned another family vacation. Maureen had found a cottage on the "sunrise" side of the state, right on Lake Huron near Alpena. This time it would be a small group that included Mom, Maureen, Dick, Megan, Matthew, and me. Pat, Patty, and Maggie would be coming for a day later in the week. We all made our way up there separately. It was June twenty-ninth.

The events that transpired during that week could not, in any sense, be defined as a vacation. There were no picnics on the beach, no splashing in the surf, no golfing, no campfires. We had one enjoyable day when we went on a boat trip around Thunder Bay. Dick loved it. It seemed he couldn't get enough of that fresh lake air. Matthew and Megan also had fun running around on the boat. Mom loved the scenery.

The plans were to spend a week in Alpena and return home for the Fourth of July. On the third evening of our stay, Dick decided that he wanted to take a little bike ride. Maureen was going to go with him, but he insisted that he could go by himself. Maureen didn't want to smother him. She knew he needed to feel some sense of independence and not rely on people for everything. Yet, we both had nagging doubts about this particular undertaking.

We cleaned up the dinner dishes and sat down for a few minutes. Dick had been gone for an hour, and it was beginning to get dark. We became concerned. Mom stayed with Matthew and Megan while Maureen, and I took the car out to look for Dick. I was driving. We drove the roads up and down around the cabin for approximately twenty minutes. It was completely dark by this time. As we were making a loop back towards the cabin, I heard Maureen say, "Oh my God!" On the right shoulder of the road straight ahead was a mere shadow of a man, limping, walking his bike. When we reached Dick, he was muddy from head to toe, and crying. Maureen jumped out of the car and ran to him. He had such a bewildered look on his face, and at the same time, you could tell he was angry. He managed to choke out, "I can't even ride my bike anymore...."

We loaded him and the bike in the car, took him back to the cabin, and Maureen gave him a nice, warm shower. Things would not get any better however, and I've often thought that the trip was the turning point in Dick's courageous battle against this monster that had settled in his brain. It would not be stopped; it was not going to go away.

During the next two days, Dick's bladder function also took a turn for the worse, and the day before we were scheduled to leave, he had an excruciating headache. None of his medications was making a difference, and Dick seemed to be lapsing in and out of consciousness. An ambulance was called, and he was taken to a nearby hospital. They stabilized him enough to feel confident he could make the two-hour journey back to the hospital near his home where he had received treatment since his diagnosis. Maureen went with him. Pat and Patty packed up the cabin and took Megan with them to a family camp in Alpena. Matt, Mom, and I headed home to Lansing.

CAT scans and MRIs revealed everyone's worst fears: the chemotherapy and radiation had only postponed the inevitable. The tumor was growing. More pain killers and steroids were prescribed.

By the end of August, Dick was in a wheelchair most of the time. He could stand up with a walker and walk for short distances. There was no shortage of care for Dick. His children, Jeri, Jill, and Scott, were out to "the farm" often, as were the McGlincheys and Dick's siblings. Dick's many friends also came to visit and lend a helping hand. Without a doubt, though, it was Megan that warmed his heart. He would sit by the window every afternoon as she jumped off the school bus fresh from her pre-school afternoon. Once when Jack was there sitting with him, Megan came running up to the house. Dick smiled and said, "Here comes my pride and joy." Megan's usual practice was to run in the house, jump in his lap and greet him with a hug. In turn Dick would take her for a ride in the wheelchair.

In early September, Matthew and I drove down for one of our many visits. It was beginning to feel like fall, and there were many jobs to be done. One of them was to close up their above-ground swimming pool for the winter. Dick was going to help by giving us the verbal instructions. We wheeled him outside, and he managed to give us a few initial instructions on how to drain some of the water out of the pool. Before too long, it was obvious that he was getting frustrated because he couldn't remember all of the steps. He became visibly upset and asked that we please take him back inside. This was the first indication of more severe "processing" problems, and his condition began to deteriorate rapidly, beginning in late September.

Around this time, we held our annual family birthday party for Matthew and Megan and my nieces Theresa and Maggie and nephew, Mark. It was a good reason to bring the extended family together to celebrate. Everyone gathered at our house, and we had a great dinner. At the same time, our attention and concern centered on Dick. When it came time to serve the cake, Dick was sitting at the dining room table. I couldn't help but notice that he was having a great deal of difficulty feeding himself. His hands were shaking badly, and he would try to steady one hand with the other as he lifted the fork to his mouth. What had happened to this wonderful man who, just months before, was a fit, happy, witty man? Damn this thing, this tumor that was stealing him away from us. However, the moment at hand dictated that one of us needed to step in and feed Dick.

We visited Dick and Maureen's many times during the next month and observed, in horror, his decline. The plans were to gather at their house on Thanksgiving so Dick could be comfortable and we wouldn't have to move him. When I arrived on Thanksgiving morning, my brother-in-law, Peter, was standing in the kitchen stuffing the turkey. There was no sign of Dick or Maureen. Apparently, Dick had been tortured by terrible seizures that morning, and he was rushed to the hospital. They would be there the entire day. This was definitely not going to be a Thanksgiving to remember. We went through the motions that day, with Dick and Maureen on our minds the entire time. Later in the evening, we took dinner to them at the hospital. I detested this thing that had dared to rear its ugly head on a day such as this. We all went back to our homes knowing that our days with Dick were numbered.

All these events were beginning to test my faith. Why couldn't we have a Thanksgiving together without a catastrophe? Where was God? Why was this happening to us? Why were we being prevented, as a family, from gathering and spending an enjoyable Thanksgiving together?

We continued to visit Maureen and Dick and help with all the tasks related to Christmas. It was decided that Pat and Patty would host our Christmas celebration at their home. They lived approximately twenty minutes from Dick and Maureen. After dinner at Pat and Patty's, we would take Christmas dinner to Dick and Maureen's and have dessert at their house.

By early December, Dick had virtually no ability to move by himself. He could be lifted out of bed and could sit in a wheelchair for a limited amount of time. At the end of December, he was confined to his bed. He had been moved to the guest bedroom on the main floor and had a hospital bed. They had the bathroom remodeled so it was wheelchair-accessible.

So this is where we gathered on that Christmas evening in 1993. Mom had flown to Michigan from Florida because we felt she needed to see Dick. She hadn't seen him since she had returned to Florida in the early fall.

Somehow or other, I had gained a reputation over the years for making good pies, so I am the official "pie baker" in the family. The favorite is my apple pie, and Dick always loved it, too. When it came time to serve dessert, Maureen asked Dick what kind of pie he wanted. Without hesitation, he replied, "Apple." She went to the kitchen to get his pie, returned to the bedroom, and began to feed him. After the first bite, he got a little twinkle in his eye, looked at me, and said "Better than sex." We all laughed, and Maureen just smiled and laughed with us.

Mom sat with Dick most of the time, holding his hand. Dick wouldn't let go of her hand, and she commented to us that it was so much like Dad when he was sick.

My mother is a devout Catholic. She is the most spiritual person I have ever met. We sat and prayed the rosary with her every night during her stay. She left a few days after Christmas, and it would be the last time she would see Dick.

As with Thanksgiving, we passed the Christmas holiday with mixed feelings. We were happy for the celebration of the birth of our savior, yet we were deeply saddened as we watched our beloved Dick move ever so quickly toward death. I visited Dick one more time as the year became 1994. It was a quiet evening, and I was the only one there with Maureen and Dick. I went into the bedroom to spend some time with him. He was sleeping most of the time now, yet somehow I think he felt my presence. I put the rosary that was on the table underneath Dick's pillow, kissed him, and said goodbye. I walked into the room next door, sat down, and cried. Maureen came in and hugged me, and it seemed the only thing we could do was to try and find comfort in each other.

Dick's kids celebrated his birthday on January fifth very quietly with him. He turned fifty-two. On Friday, January 14, 1994, Dick died. The priest who had visited him on the day of his death had a compelling feeling that he needed to see Dick. A Mass was being celebrated on television when he died. Maureen and his children were there with him.

⬛⬛⬛⬛

I was playing cards at my neighbor's house when my brother called to tell me about Dick's death. I sat down and finished the few hands that were left to play. Dick would have wanted it that way. He loved it when people were together. More importantly, I was not alone, and I was able to be comforted by my husband and friends. I was going to drive to Maureen's house that night, but it was ten o'clock p.m. when Pat called, and it was a typical January night in Michigan. I would wait until the next morning.

When I crawled into bed that night, Mark held me, and I cried. I wasn't concerned about Dick anymore. I knew he was no longer suffering and was "new" again ... and much happier than he was at any time here, on earth. I was just so sad for the passing of such a great man and for Maureen and his kids, especially little Megan. He was leaving such a void that no other person could possibly fill. I considered the beast that claimed him. I had witnessed, first hand, the ugliness of cancer. What an insidious beast. It reminded me of a playground bully that picks on children much smaller and younger. The victims are rendered helpless. Cancer seemed so much bigger than Dick ... so much bigger than so many people.

I did not sleep well that night because my mind would not shut down. I pulled myself out of bed before sunrise and made the hour-and-a-half drive to Maureen's. I arrived as the sun was rising, and I entered what I thought was an empty house. There was no sign of Megan in her room. I went to Dick and Maureen's room, and Maureen was still in bed. I crawled in bed with her, and we held onto each other and cried. Words were meaningless.

I spent the next three days at Maureen's house, as did most of the family. We went to the funeral home to help her make the arrangements, pick out a casket, and clean the house for a gathering after the funeral. Mark stayed back in Lansing with Matthew and joined us for the funeral.

On the day of the funeral, the temperature was close to zero. On that frigid day, we said goodbye to Dick, the man we all loved so dearly. Gone was his beautiful smile. Gone was his witty personality and wonderful ability to make people laugh. We all wept as we followed him outside the church, and as he was loaded in the hearse. We said our final goodbyes there, as the hearse pulled him away to be cremated.

After the funeral, Margie and I decided to take Maureen and Megan to an inside resort in Canada called "Wheels Inn." Matthew and Megan would have a great time, and we could give Maureen the rest and relaxation she needed. They also had a spa where she could make an appointment for a facial and a massage. We played Scrabble, swam, exercised, relaxed, and cried *often*. And so we began our time of grief for the passing of the fun-loving man we already missed tremendously. I had no understanding that our grief was just beginning and that we would continue to grieve for quite some time.

Maureen

Two weeks after Dick's death, Maureen was scheduled for a routine mammogram. She had always been conscientious about breast exams. When she was in her twenties, she had to have two non-cancerous lumps removed. Since that time, she had monitored her breast health closely. As a matter of fact, she was involved in a breast study program at a university hospital.

When she received a call that something "suspicious" was picked up on her mammogram, we were not overly concerned. She was scheduled for a wire localization. A thin wire would be threaded through the breast tissue where the calcification or density was picked up on the mammogram. The surgeon would remove the tissue around the wire. This procedure ensures that the suspicious tissue is indeed being biopsied, rather than random breast tissue.

The biopsy was scheduled for late January. Jeri drove Maureen to the hospital, and I met them there. I remember sitting in the hospital before she was taken back to get ready for the biopsy. We were convinced that it was only a calcification. We had all experienced these false alarms before and were told to "cut down on caffeine, eat a healthy diet, get plenty of exercise, and basically live a healthy lifestyle." They wheeled

Maureen in for a biopsy and Jeri and I could think of only one thing to do: pray fervently.

When Maureen did not hear from the doctor after a week, she finally called. I considered it a good sign that she had not heard from him. If the news was bad, certainly she would have heard before a week had passed. Apparently, the doctor had been out of town for a few days, which caused the delay. After being told the results of the biopsy, she called my house and spoke to Mark because I was not at home. When I came home, Mark was standing in the kitchen and told me she had called with the news. It was cancer. I remember my response was total disbelief. Certainly, the doctors must be mistaken. How could she have cancer? Hadn't we just been through this?

I went for a long, fast walk. As I walked, I talked with God, and discussed how despondent I was. I had read the poem entitled "Footprints" many times before and wondered if God had accidentally dropped us. The poem speaks of two sets of footprints in the sand; eventually the two sets of prints become one, and that is when God is carrying those with heavy burdens. All through Dad's and Dick's illnesses, I prayed for things not to be bad. Could Dad just go quickly after he had his stroke, and not suffer? Apparently not. Please, could Dick have a treatable type of brain tumor? Apparently not. Could he go peacefully and quickly and not suffer? Apparently not. I tried praying to the patron saint of cancer and the patron saint of lost causes, and I prayed my rosary often. Why wasn't anyone listening? Were my prayers not good enough? What in the hell was happening to us?

Certainly this time things would be different. I had to believe that, or I was at risk of not being able to function at all. When the doctor called with the news, he said Maureen would be scheduled for a lumpectomy and lymph node surgery. Jeri knew a fine doctor in the hospital in which she worked who would do the surgery.

Once again, in the early morning on a mid-February day, we gathered in the hospital. This time we were in Pontiac, Michigan. Jack, Margie, Jeri, Chris, and I sat and waited while the procedure was being done. The doctor said it would take from one to three hours. When the surgeon wasn't out in three hours, we began to wonder what was taking so long. Just after noon, the surgeon came into the waiting room and directed us into a consultation room. After greeting us, he began his discussion with, "How I wish I had better news for you." I hardly heard much more. He said something about enlarged lymph nodes that looked like little peas. The rest was a blur.

Margie and Jack were clinging to one another, and Jack kept saying, "Oh my God, it's not good." They were both crying, and I had my head between my knees. The room was reeling, and I was going to pass out.

It took me awhile to recover. Margie and I walked out to the hallway, and I sent the paper basket by the elevator flying across the floor. My shock had turned to anger. Why? Why was this happening? Had our prayers fallen on deaf ears again? What about the sweet little girl whose Daddy had just died who was waiting for Mommy to come home? Where was the care and compassion for her?

We stayed until Maureen recovered from anesthesia. She had one question when she woke up. We told her the results weren't conclusive until the lab reports came back. There was a chance that the doctors had made a terrible mistake ... there had to be that slight chance! None of us wanted to tell her what they thought.

The drive home from Pontiac was quiet and reflective. I could feel myself sinking in disbelief. Sadness and fear overwhelmed me. I dragged myself inside the house and hugged Mark and Matthew and told Mark the most recent developments. He, too, could not believe it.

In my exhausted state, I climbed the steps to my bedroom, fell on my knees, and sobbed. With tears rolling down my cheeks, I begged and pleaded with God to spare Maureen and to lead us in the direction of a cure. We needed her. More importantly, Megan needed her. There were so many people out there who had made a mockery of their lives ... murderers, rapists, people who had done nothing in their lives to improve society. How about one of them? Simplistic as it may sound, I was ready to make some deals with God. I would do anything to spare this jewel, my sister, who had taught me so much and brought endless joy to my life and the lives of so many others.

A few days later, the biopsy revealed some serious problems. Later, in one of Maureen's cancer information books, I found her handwritten notes: "Extensive, intraductal cancer, invasive throughout the breast, in the lymph nodes. Some cancer in the area of the lymph nodes ... rarely see this. Need to be concerned about the liver, lungs and bones ... will be treated as inflammatory breast cancer."

And so we became very familiar with a new treatment protocol. This time, rather than a brain tumor, it was breast cancer. Maureen saw a leading breast cancer specialist at Harper Hospital in Detroit. She would receive three months of strong chemotherapy "cocktails," Adriamycin, Methotrexate, and others, in an effort to get the cancer cells under control. Following the chemotherapy, she would have a mastectomy. She would have radiation treatments and possibly more chemotherapy when she recovered from the mastectomy, which was usually six weeks.

As Maureen's condition became clearer, I was having a difficult time coping and coming to terms with the fact that she, too, was fighting for her life. I was having trouble eating and sleeping. She was on my mind constantly. I went to my doctor and told her what had happened in my life during the past few months. She, very wisely, suggested that I would need some help getting through this traumatic time and gave me the name of a psychologist. I had never been to a psychologist before, but I couldn't get there fast enough.

It turned out that Karen, the psychologist, was exactly what I needed. She had just lost a dear friend from breast cancer. She validated everything I was feeling. We cried together. Most importantly, she made me realize that there were no "normal" feelings for the losses I had experienced. I would be re-defining normal and abnormal reactions to events I would experience in the future. My goal was to survive, with God's help and the help of my friends and family. I had to remain strong ... and yet at the same time allow myself to feel bad, sad, angry, and whatever else I wanted to feel.

Maureen's treatment began immediately. She had her first chemotherapy treatment at the end of February, 1994. By St. Patrick's Day, most of her hair had fallen out. We had been shopping for a wig the week before, and she wore it for the first time to a St. Patrick's Day party.

She did not seem to be bothered by the chemotherapy. It did not make her sick or decrease her appetite or energy. As a matter of fact, prior to her diagnosis, she had applied for a new job, interviewed, and was offered the job as an assistant director at a women's shelter. She took the job because she felt she needed to stay busy and it would keep her mind off the cancer and help her to focus on more productive things.

I went with Maureen for her second chemotherapy treatment. She received the chemo through a port that was surgically implanted in her chest. It frightened me to be there. I saw people that looked like they were extremely ill. I wondered why they were receiving treatments in the same area as Maureen. She still looked healthy. Did the sight of these people also scare her? I decided that she couldn't have been too bothered by them. On the way home, we stopped at Wendy's. Maureen ordered a baked potato with chili on top of it. I choked down a salad.

In mid-April, Maureen caught some type of virus and became sick. She had a temperature and was in bed for two days. I was one of her "nurses" during that time. It was then that I observed the nosebleeds, the upset stomachs, the chills. We called the doctor, and he prescribed something ... and told us to feed her lots of yogurt with acidophilus, Jell-

O, and chicken noodle soup. Maureen recovered, but the illness was a red flag for me. Although Maureen didn't look it, she was frail and walking on the edge every day.

Maureen's mastectomy was scheduled in mid-May, after her blood counts improved from her third chemotherapy treatment. Once again, we all gathered in the visitors waiting room outside of the surgery ward. She was having the mastectomy done closer to home at a neighboring hospital. We spent our time rotating between the waiting room and the chapel.

After what seemed like days, the surgeon emerged from the operating room to tell us the surgery went well. She said the breast came off cleanly with no visible signs of disease, but we wouldn't know the true results until the pathology report came back. The plastic surgeon was still working on Maureen. She had decided after a discussion with the doctor to have reconstructive surgery. She would have an expander placed where her breast used to be. Over the course of six months, she would visit the doctor to have the sack "expanded" with saline solution. Gradually, her tissue and muscle would expand so she would feel little discomfort and, in the end, have a "breast."

It wasn't long before the plastic surgeon was finished and emerged to give us the report that everything had gone smoothly. The recovery could begin now. Maureen would heal and begin her last phase of treatment in six weeks. She would have a series of radiation treatments to complete the process. It was all downhill from here, wasn't it?

Once again, the answer was "apparently not." When the pathology report came back from the surgeon, it was discovered that the breast did not come off "cleanly." There were cancer cells found on the outside margins of the breast tissue, which meant that there were cancer cells on Maureen's chest wall where the breast had been removed. I was disgusted, afraid, petrified, angry, furious, and losing hope. Would this ever end?

During the next few weeks, we got together with Maureen often. She looked great, healed quickly, and remained positive. We actually went out on the golf course a few times to bang the ball around. She was scheduled for a radiation simulation in late June. The radiologist met her and consulted with her first, then scheduled the simulation.

⁂

Fortunately, before any more treatment would take place, we were able to escape to a family resort in Canada called Evergreen. Pat, Patty, Maggie, Maureen, Megan, Margie, Molly, Matthew, Grandma, and I excitedly piled in our cars to make the trip. Pat and Patty had been there many times before and had told us what a great place it was for kids. Their assessment of Evergreen was correct. It provided all types of activities for adults and children in a peaceful setting on the Canadian side of Lake Huron. Once you are "in" at Evergreen, you can vacation during the same week every year. Our week became the first full week from Saturday to Saturday after the Fourth of July. Eventually, you get to know most, if not all, of the families that attend during your week. You become reacquainted with your friends every summer, and it's almost as if you never left. Time seems to stand still there. The kids absolutely loved it and to this day, count down the days all year to report how many days there are until "Evergreen." During our week in 1994, Maureen had to leave on Wednesday to get back for something at work. Megan stayed behind with us to finish the week. Maureen also had to get ready for her radiation appointment the following week.

The simulation was supposed to be a routine procedure. The radiologist took many measurements and new x-rays and CAT scans. Imagine Maureen's surprise when he came into the room and announced that he couldn't do radiation treatments on her because she had a metal device in her chest. Her reply was, "What are you talking about?" Sure enough, apparently the plastic surgeon had used an implant with a wire in it to help form the shape of her new breast. Apparently there was a lack of communication between the oncologist, the plastic surgeon, and the radiologist concerning what type of implant should be used according to Maureen's specific treatment protocol. Regardless, the implant had to come out.

The implant was removed in early August in an outpatient procedure. Maureen was so disappointed. She had just begun to gradually have the implant filled and was feeling as if her body was at last looking more normal every day. After the procedure, Maureen's chest looked like it had gone through a great war. It was badly scarred, and now there was a hole where the plastic surgeon had removed the implant. Supposedly, it would close and heal over time.

It never did. As a matter of fact, she developed an infection that started at the site and spread to her arm. It was swollen and red. She waited until it was throbbing before she returned to the doctor. I'm sure she was hoping and praying her body would fight the infection. I'm sure she was tired of doctors and hospitals.

She was admitted into the hospital and given massive doses of an antibiotic. It was now late August. She had the mastectomy in May, and instead of beginning radiation after six weeks, we were past eight weeks and there would be no radiation until the infection cleared. I am not a physician, but I couldn't help but wonder: if there was even a slight risk of an infection, which would delay further treatment, why would an implant even be suggested? Maureen was struggling to stay alive.

Just as I was beginning to feel better about Maureen's condition, the hopeful feeling quickly faded. I had just started school again. I knew I had some "end of summer, going back to school blues" but this was more than that. I visited Karen, my psychologist, again. She listened to the most recent developments and suggested we see each other more regularly until things stabilized again. She prescribed some drugs to help me sleep and relieve some of the anxiety I was experiencing. I took them sparingly and only when I felt overwhelmed by the anxiety and feelings of despair. Maureen's illness was definitely causing great emotional turmoil for me. During one appointment with Karen, we discussed acupuncture treatments. I was willing to try any alternative to drug therapy. As it turned out, the treatments seemed to calm me and settle my digestive system.

I also needed to seek help now in a spiritual sense. I had continued to sing in the choir and attend Mass every week, but to say I felt abandoned would be an understatement. Why wasn't God listening to me? I went to see the pastor of our church, who was a very wise, Irish bishop. I explained the situation to him and told him that my praying, begging, and pleading had made no difference in the chain of events that began with Dad's illness. I had reached the point where I was afraid to pray. I remember Father Murray's response perfectly. He said, "I'll tell you what ... why don't you quit praying for awhile? In the meantime, I'll pray for you on behalf of your sister. It's one of the things I'm pretty good at, and I'll get all my friends in higher places to help me." As strange as it may sound, that was exactly what I needed to hear. If my prayers couldn't save Maureen, perhaps the prayers of Father Murray and all his friends would help. If their prayers weren't good enough, it was time for me to look at things from a different perspective. Perhaps my prayers were good enough and God had a different plan for all of us.

Maureen's infection finally began to clear up in mid-September. The doctor could wait no longer, and radiation began at that time. More than three months had passed since Maureen's mastectomy. We were not even close to the recommended time frame of beginning radiation six weeks after a mastectomy

In every other way, we attempted to retain some degree of normalcy in our lives. Theresa, my niece, and Craig, her fiancé, would be married in November, so we had planned a wedding shower in September to be held at Maureen's house. We all contributed to the shower in whatever way we could. We all enjoyed a happy celebration for a change.

As Megan began school that September, it became apparent that Maureen would need some help. Megan was just beginning first grade. Maureen's longtime Suttons Bay friend came through to offer assistance in a big way. Her name was Sharon, and her daughter, Chaesa, was just beginning her college career and had agreed to move in with Maureen to help with Megan's care. Chaesa attended classes during the day while Megan was in school, which would allow her to be with Megan in the evenings. She was a wonderful help to Maureen and Megan.

In early October, Maureen, Margie, Megan, Molly, Matthew, and I attended a "We Can" weekend retreat for cancer patients and their families. There were different sessions offered for adults, and many activities were also scheduled for the children. We arrived on Friday evening, registered, and walked the grounds. The following morning, we attended sessions and participated in most of the activities throughout the day. Without a doubt, the most memorable event that weekend was the kids' parade. Each child had decorated a victory banner. We have a photograph of Megan during the parade, carrying her flag. The expression on her face is, indeed, triumphant. She was glowing. It remains one on my favorite photos of her to this day.

Later in the evening, Maureen had to go to work for awhile to attend a fundraising event for the women's shelter. Margie and I played with the kids and put them to bed around nine. I was up reading a book when Maureen returned.

I remember that after we sat and talked for a few minutes, Maureen mentioned that she wanted to talk about Megan. I asked, "What about Megan?" Maureen replied that she wanted to talk about Megan in the event that things didn't go as we hoped and prayed and she didn't survive. I cut her off. My reply was, "Maureen, I can't talk about this now. If I do, it's as if I'm allowing the cancer to take control, or admitting that you're not going to make it. I can't give up hope. By discussing an alternative future for Megan other than the life she has with you, that's exactly what I'm doing. When the doctors tell you there's absolutely no hope and you're going to die, maybe then we can talk." Maureen just kind of shrugged her shoulders and agreed. In retrospect, I regret that I was never really able to have that conversation with her. I just couldn't believe, even as things deteriorated, that she might die.

Megan proudly displaying her flag during the children's
parade at the "We Can" Cancer Support Weekend.

In November, we were all busy planning for Theresa and Craig's wedding. Theresa was Jack's only daughter, so he spared no expense for the wedding. The church ceremony was beautiful and the reception was held at an elegant hall in Sterling Heights, Michigan. It was gorgeously decorated for Christmas. We were all so happy. Maureen's hair had begun to grow back. Her radiation treatments were done. Her beauty and healthy demeanor seemed to define the evening for us. Ed did some singing, everyone was dancing, and we took what seemed like hundreds of pictures in the front entryway next to a huge, beautifully-decorated Christmas tree. How could we have known that it would be our last joyous occasion for a very long time?

On the weekend of my December 10th birthday, Maureen and Margie came to Lansing, and we shopped. They bought me a blue jean jumper that I had wanted for a long time. As always, time with them was memorable and treasured. What I remember most about the day, however, was that Maureen was having pain in her back. She was pretty sure she had twisted it as she was getting down her Christmas decorations. She looked very uncomfortable.

The next weekend, Margie, Maureen, and I had planned to take the kids to a "Sesame Street Live" show at the Fox Theater in Detroit. We met in Wixom, a little town not far from Maureen's house, so we could carpool together. As we watched Maureen move from the driver's seat, it was obvious that she was still in great discomfort. When we arrived at the Fox Theater, and before attempting to get out of the car, Maureen announced that she would need a wheelchair. Margie and I stared at each other in disbelief. A wheelchair? We knew what a wheelchair symbolized. We had seen it with Dick and Dad. It represented the beginning of a quick downward spiral, the beginning of the end. It represented the end of a carefree life, of independence, of freedom. The wheelchair represented an ominous sign of impending tragedy.

We didn't let Maureen see the tears streaming down our faces as we loaded her into the wheelchair and pushed her into the theater to see the show. We pretended to enjoy the show, not wanting Maureen or the kids to know that our thoughts were miles away ... and filled with great fear of what the future might hold. On the way out of the show, we discovered that someone had stolen Maureen's wallet-type purse. Fortunately, with the help of the theater staff, we located it outside the building. Her health insurance and credit cards were still inside the wallet. The $70 in cash was gone. How could someone steal from a person in a wheelchair? It was more personal because it was my sister, and she was obviously suffering from cancer. In spite of the incident, we managed to get Maureen home, and then Margie and I made our way back to Kalamazoo and Lansing.

I called Maureen numerous times during the next week. Her back seemed to be improving with the help of some pain medication, but more X-rays and CAT scans were ordered. It was a week before Christmas, 1994. We were hoping for the best and praying for good news. The good news came three days before Christmas. Apparently, Maureen had developed "hot spots" on her spine due to the radiation treatments. She had left a message on my answering machine. I was elated, as was she.

The next two days went by blissfully. I finished last-minute Christmas details, and on Christmas Eve, the kitchen became a baker's paradise. The aroma of apple, pumpkin, and other fruit pies filled the kitchen.. Mark, Matthew, and I enjoyed a special dinner. We went for our traditional Christmas Eve walk in the neighborhood and came home and listened to Raffi's Christmas music with Matthew. I was bursting with the joy of Christmas as I made my way to my car at ten o'clock p.m. for my choral warm-up for Christmas Eve Mass.

The following morning, we watched with sheer delight as our six-year-old unwrapped his Christmas presents. He was especially fond of his Playmobile castle. We opened the rest of the gifts and then quickly got ready to make our way to Kalamazoo for our family Christmas gathering at Peter and Margie's house.

It was unbelievably warm in Michigan on that Christmas Day, 1994. The temperature was close to sixty degrees. When we arrived at Margie's house, I burst into the house yelling, "Merry Christmas!" with pies and gifts in my hands. It was very quiet inside the house. Margie was in the kitchen cooking. She announced that the "boys" had all gone golfing. They couldn't resist the opportunity to play golf in Michigan on Christmas morning. The kids were downstairs, and Maureen was taking a nap.

As Margie bent over the oven, she asked if Maureen had called me yesterday. I replied that she hadn't. It was then that I noticed that Margie didn't look like she was filled with Christmas cheer. On the contrary, she looked sad and reflective. "What's wrong?" I asked. She couldn't tell me before the tears stared flowing. The doctors had done some further testing. Maureen was told the evening before Christmas Eve that the spots were not radiation "hot spots" and that her cancer had spread to her spine.

I wanted to run away screaming. I wanted to hit something. I melted on the floor in a heap of despair. Why today? Why any day? Why was the news bad *again?* Didn't we spend last Christmas nursing Dick and trying to pretend that we were having a "merry" Christmas, knowing that he probably only had a few days to live? Obviously, this would not be a happy family gathering after all. There was someone in our midst who was suffering, and we would all suffer as a result. It all seemed so unfair.

Maureen woke up from her nap. We talked, we cried, but she was as determined as ever. This was a setback. There was still tomorrow. New treatments would be tried—more aggressive chemotherapy. The boys returned from golf, and we had our Christmas dinner. Afterwards, we opened presents. We tried very hard to be celebratory.

***

A week later, we gathered in Maureen's living room to set up a schedule for her care. Chaesa had to move to continue her education, which meant that we would have to step in to help Maureen more often. There were enough of us, including her step-daughter, Jeri, to provide continuous care for her. Margie was pregnant and would help on the weekends when she could. My turn to help would be on Tuesday afternoon and evening until Wednesday afternoon. I planned to make the hour-and-a-half drive to her house on Tuesday after getting out of school. I took some sick days I could use to care for family members for the Wednesday mornings I would be gone. As we sat in a circle in Maureen's living room, I remember that it was one of the few times I saw her cry through the whole ordeal. She apologized for "disrupting our lives." I assured her that the arrangements we were making were only temporary and that she would be well again in no time. She didn't look convinced.

When Maureen saw her oncologist again a few days later with some family members, it was decided that she would go to the University of Michigan and be evaluated for a possible bone marrow transplant. The appointment was scheduled for mid-January. On the day of the appointment, I had an important teacher training in-service, so Margie and Jack accompanied Maureen to her appointment. I called Margie later that day and learned what had transpired at the hospital during the day. None of it was good. She said she sensed that the doctors thought a lot of time had been wasted that day, because Maureen was way beyond a bone marrow transplant. Her cancer was too advanced.

The next few weeks went by quickly. We had begun our schedule of assistance for Maureen. I relived Pat, my sister-in-law on Tuesday afternoons. I usually left school early. I would make dinner for Maureen and Megan, and basically be on call for the evening. Jack arrived at three in the morning after his shift at work. He would go to sleep, then arise at mid-morning on Wednesday as I got ready to return to school. Other family members and friends filled in the rest of the week. Maureen started a new regimen of chemotherapy drugs, as well as high doses of pain medication. The time we spent together was both unsettling and memorable. It was unsettling because it was obvious that Maureen was not getting better.

Although Megan never specifically asked about Maureen's prognosis, she was very wise for a seven-year-old. She had seen it all before with her dad. So we tried to make Tuesday evenings as special as possible. We would have dinner, read books, help Megan with her homework, and watch TV. Megan would cuddle with Maureen on the sofa as she read her many bedtime stories. Megan was a smart kid. She was already a fluent reader mid-way through her first grade year. So, when Maureen got tired of reading to Megan, Megan would read to her mom. It was so precious to watch her. Eventually, I'd put Megan to bed upstairs and then begin my night duty with Maureen.

In retrospect, we all laugh about the bell that Maureen used to alert us when she needed help. It was a doorbell that played the University of Michigan fight song. It's funny because it drove us crazy and also because Maureen was never a University of Michigan fan. Perhaps she was trying to turn all of us against the "Wolverines." Anyway, Maureen slept in the same downstairs room where Dick had died. It had become very difficult for her to negotiate the steps to her upstairs bedroom. Although there was another full-sized bed in addition to a hospital bed, I slept in the living room on a makeshift bed on the floor. Maureen was having trouble falling asleep, so she used to watch TV until the wee hours of the morning. I needed to get at least a little bit of sleep, which was why I was in the next room on the floor. Maureen would ring the doorbell many times. Often just before I'd nod off to sleep, the doorbell would ring, and I'd run to assist her in some way.

In spite of the "bell," the time was memorable as Maureen, Megan, and I and their dog, Cody, became a small part-time family. We tried to maintain some sense of normalcy amidst the uncertainty of each tomorrow.

And so it continued until we all gathered together at Maureen's house on that Sunday in late February, 1995, bearing gifts to celebrate her forty-seventh birthday. She looked tired and uncomfortable during most of the day. She opened her presents, and we had cake and ice cream. The only time she looked happy was when little Megan slipped her feet into her tiny Irish step dancing shoes. Maureen clapped to the music and smiled as Megan danced on the living room floor. There was magic in her feet. For a short time, the pain, the cancer, the burdens were gone. We were a big, happy family again. When the music and dancing stopped, reality returned. We all went home with the exception of my brother Ed, who stayed with Maureen and Megan.

It was the following morning, when I had settled in for that February twenty-sixth "snow day" that the phone rang and I was told Maureen had developed breathing problems and Jack and Ed were headed for the hospital with her. I made that trip from my house to Harper Hospital with a sense of dread. Given my experiences in the past, I knew that whatever was wrong, it was not going to be good news. I waited in the waiting room and met them in the drive-up entrance when they arrived. When she was taken up to the room, I went with her and gave her the permission to "just go, when she got tired of fighting." She looked so tired and defeated. When her response was, "Are you kidding? I just keep offering this up to God," I was relieved. She was as determined as ever to keep fighting. More tests and scans were ordered, and we all waited for the results.

Later, when I joined the boys in the lobby, we had a malpractice discussion. It seemed to us that many mistakes had been made over the course of Maureen's treatment, especially concerning her delayed diagnosis and the implant error. Jack, however, had already had the discussion with Maureen. We were looking for a reason for her current condition and to place blame somewhere and with someone. When one considers Maureen's personality, her reaction was not surprising. She said something like this: "A lawsuit would make a mockery of my life and all I've tried to do. This is no one's fault. Everyone who has treated me has tried to stop this." That was the end of the discussion. We never talked about litigation again.

The following day we received the grave news that in spite of new, aggressive chemotherapy, Maureen's cancer was continuing to spread. She was having difficulty breathing because the cancer had spread to her sternum. Things were not getting better—they were getting worse.

Maureen was sent home the following day. She would take stronger doses of morphine, and she would continue to receive chemotherapy in a continuous drip from a pack that was strapped around her waist. At this point, everything was done in an effort to slow down the out-of-control cancer and to make her comfortable. At the same time, she was still getting around quite well, although she would tire quickly and needed frequent naps.

We were still assisting her at our assigned "shift" times, and the damned doorbell continued to let us know when she needed help at night. I remember one night in particular when I was especially tired, it was well past midnight, and the "bell" had already rung a few times. I was exhausted and aware that Megan would need help in the morning. It was around one-thirty a.m., and just as I was nodding off to sleep I was startled awake by the bell again. When I stumbled into the room, Maureen asked me to move the table closer to her bed. I snapped back, "What could you possibly want off of the table at one-thirty a.m.?"

She replied, "Never mind, I'll get it myself!" as she attempted to rise and stumble out of bed.

I grabbed the table, slammed it down next to the bed, and said, "Don't ring that bell again! I need to get some sleep!" I turned around and walked back to my makeshift bed on the floor.

Sleep however, did not come. My thoughts centered on what I had just done. I began to think Maureen would fall asleep and die, and that would be our last interaction together. Why was I concerned about a little sleep when she was slowly progressing toward death? After a few minutes, I went back to Maureen, crying, and told her I was sorry. We exchanged "I love you's" and a few tears. I stayed with her until there was nothing else to watch on TV and she fell asleep. I managed to catch a couple hours of sleep, got Megan off to school, and then went to school myself.

Soon, another St. Patrick's Day was on the horizon. It had been only a year since we were all at a St. Patrick's Day party with Maureen. She had just begun treatment, and her hair had fallen out. It was the first time she had worn her wig. Celebrating St. Patrick's Day in our traditional manner would not be possible this year. I believe it was actually Maureen's idea to get a hotel room not far from her home so everyone could "get away" for a night. The kids could swim, and we could all relax as much as possible.

Although it sounded like a good idea, it didn't turn out very well. Our rooms were not ready when we arrived about four p.m. We waited and waited. Maureen was getting very tired and needed to take a nap. I think it was close to six p.m. before we finally got into one room and put her to bed for a nap. The rest of us went out by the pool, had dinner, and watched the kids swim. Maggie, Megan, Matthew, and Molly were having a great time. Later that evening, it became apparent that Maureen was having trouble getting settled in her new surroundings. She couldn't rest and felt uncomfortable being away from home. It was around eleven p.m. when we loaded her into the car. I drove her back home and stayed with her. Everyone else remained at the hotel and came back to Maureen's house the following afternoon.

The next two weeks passed uneventfully. I had parent-teacher conferences during the last week of March. Spring break would follow during the first week of April. I spent my Tuesday night with Maureen and prepared to leave around eleven a.m. to get back to school by one p.m. for conferences. Jeri came out to the house earlier and was there as I got dressed. I remember having a discussion with her about Maureen's eyes. The whites of her eyes were beginning to turn yellow. Jeri explained that the cancer was obviously spreading to her liver. Our days with Maureen were numbered.

Spring break was traditionally a time to fly to Florida and spend a week at Mom's house. I had decided long ago, however, that I would not be going to Florida this year. I spent most of the week with Maureen while Mark took care of himself and Matthew at home.

With the exception of the pain killers, all cancer treatment for Maureen was stopped. It was not making a difference. She knew, as did we, that there would be no miraculous cure for her. We all had to come to the realization that she could not defeat the beast. It had taken Dick, and it would take Maureen, too.

Unbelievably, I think Maureen remained somewhat oblivious to the severity of her condition. I remember one Tuesday morning, as I was feeding her breakfast, she made some comment about the fact that people often felt sad after spending time with her. She asked me if she looked bad. I told her that she was as beautiful as ever. "How are you feeling?" I asked.

"Great!" she said. "Let's go outside on this beautiful sunny day." I wheeled her outside on the porch. It was a gorgeous April morning, and Easter was soon to come.

It seemed like just a few days later that we were gathered again at Maureen's house for Easter Sunday. I remember the day well, and I remember the change in Maureen. She certainly had not resigned herself to the inevitable, but there was a great determination to get things "arranged." She pulled Mark aside, and they talked for a long time. My heart ached. I knew they were talking about future arrangements involving Megan, but I didn't have the strength to ask to join in the conversation. Maureen didn't ask me either. She painfully realized she would miss all the milestones in Megan's life, yet she was determined to lay the groundwork for Megan's future. Her strength and presence of mind amazed me. I was so thankful that Mark was able to assure her that day, and I still feel guilty that I was not able to offer her the peace of mind that she so desperately needed.

Later that day, we were all sitting around in the living room, listening to music. We all talked little Megan into doing some Irish step dancing for us. She slipped on her dinky soft shoes, the music began, and her feet started flying. We were all clapping and having a grand time. I'll never forget the expression on Maureen's face as she watched Megan. It was sheer pride and joy. Gone was the cancer. Gone were the pain and suffering. Gone was the sadness. Megan had transformed the room again with her little feet. Megan had chased the beast away, not only for Maureen, but for all of us. Momentarily we were changed. It would be the last time that Megan would dance for her mother.

On the following day, I called Ele's Place, a center for grieving children and families, centered in Lansing. I needed advice. Maureen was not going to get better, and her house was becoming more and more chaotic. People were coming in and out at all times. Maureen was spending most of her time in bed. I thought that possibly Megan should be sheltered and protected from the chaos. Megan was still trying to go to school every morning amidst the confusion. Should we take her home with us and bring her for frequent visits to Maureen?

Their advice made perfect sense to me after I thought about it. They simply stated that under no circumstances should we remove Megan from her mother. She needed to be there for whatever might happen. If we took her away, Megan might feel guilty the rest of her life that she had left her mother during her time of greatest need. The reason why their advice was so practical and made perfect sense became clear. They both needed each other. Megan would read Maureen stories and "take care of her mom." She would often jump in Maureen's bed and be a silly, typical seven-year-old. Maureen loved her company. She loved her baby. There was no question that Megan needed her mom. She was devoted to her. So, Megan remained amidst the chaos with her loving mother.

A little more than a week later, I got the call I had been dreading. We had begun hospice services earlier in the month, and they were calling family members to Maureen's bedside. It appeared the end was now at hand.

Margie called me from Kalamazoo and suggested that we go to Maureen's together. She picked me up just before five p.m. We stopped to pick up a sandwich at Subway and forced ourselves to eat while we drove. We clung to each other, assuring each other that somehow, we would survive the death of our beloved older sister. But how, in God's holy name, could we?

When we arrived at Maureen's house, we were surprised to see that she had somehow made her way upstairs. Later, I was told that the boys had carried her upstairs at her request. As we walked into the room, we noticed that there were perhaps twenty people gathered around her bed. All were family or very close friends. Maureen was awake and seemed surprised by all of the attention. When I bent down to kiss her, she grabbed my hands. She appeared very weak and somewhat disoriented. We prayed for awhile, and slowly, people began to leave. By ten p.m. that night, everyone was gone, and Maureen was still with us. I got into bed with her, and we talked for awhile. Strangely enough, I asked her if she wanted me to do her nails. It was just something we did for each other now and then. She said, "Sure." Margie and I gave her a good manicure and spent "sister" time together. It seemed like such a natural thing to do.

By midnight, we were all tired. Margie, being seven months pregnant, went downstairs to sleep. I stayed upstairs and slept in the bed with Maureen. Jeri slept at the foot of the bed on a makeshift bed on the floor. Being the caring nurse that she is, I'm sure she got up two or three times to check on Maureen. Surprisingly, I slept.

When we woke up, Maureen announced that she wanted to go back downstairs. The boys, who had also spent the night, put her in a wheelchair and gently guided her downstairs. Mom arrived from Florida just as Maureen was being carried down the stairs by the boys. Maureen was so happy to see Mom, and the feeling was mutual. Mom gently put her hands around Maureen's face as she sat in the wheelchair and inquired, "How are you doing, honey?"

Maureen's response was rather humorous. "I guess I'm not doing too well." She still didn't seem to understand the severity of her condition.

A couple of hours later, we all realized that she completely understood her condition. As we sat in her living room, we were all talking about one thing or another. Suddenly, Maureen said, "You thought I was going to die last night, didn't you?" We admitted that we did, but also expressed our relief that she decided against it. She just sort of laughed and said, "Not yet."

Afterwards, I thought how appropriate that was. Maureen, like Dad, would pick the time and place. Dad was supposed to die when the doctors took him off the respirator. Instead, he chose to die at a later time and in a different place. I was so thankful Maureen decided to do the same thing and hang around awhile longer. Margie and I had many wonderful conversations with our sister the last week of her life. Most of them were quite humorous, and some were of a more serious nature. Margie and I actually considered going home to our families when Maureen rallied. I'm so glad that we didn't.

One of our humorous conversations occurred the next morning. Maureen woke up and announced, "I guess I'll marry Milt!" As mentioned earlier, Milt was Maureen's longtime friend. They loved each other. They tried to make it a "romantic" type of love at one time or another, but settled instead for a different kind of never-ending love.

Milt came that afternoon, and Margie and I told him what Maureen had said. He was shocked. Although it made no sense to Margie and me, it made perfect sense to him. Many years earlier, while they were still in college, he and Maureen had entered into a contractual agreement. The agreement stipulated that if, by a certain age, neither of them was married, they would marry each other. Milt said it was an actual, written contract that was in his basement somewhere, and he was determined that he would find it when he went home. He was surprised and touched that Maureen had remembered the agreement which spoke volumes about the type of relationship they shared.

The next morning, Maureen woke up and said, "Let's go get some big, strong, Irish, drinking men!" Margie and I just looked at each other and said, "Wow, that must have been some dream!" We told Maureen that it was a great idea, and had a great conversation centered on the topic.

At one point, we had a more serious conversation. We told Maureen that things weren't looking so good. She admitted that they were not, but also promised that she would never leave us. We were "sisters, and there were never more devoted sisters." There would be two of us in heaven,

Roseanne and Maureen. Margie and I would be left here on earth for awhile longer. We had children to raise. It soon became obvious to me that Maureen's promise to "never leave us" was more than just idle talk. I have felt her presence, in very real ways, numerous times since that day.

Before long, the weekend arrived. Husbands, wives, and children filled the house. We all took care of Maureen, and we welcomed visitors as well. On Sunday, Maureen took a turn for the worse. It was April thirtieth. Jeri was with us as well. Maureen was barely conscious in the afternoon. I got in bed with her for a little while as she lapsed in and out of consciousness. It just felt good, like old times when Margie, Maureen, and I used to all sleep in the same bed. I needed to be close to her. I got up after awhile and walked around. There were family and friends all over the house.

At some point in time, when there was a break in the devotions being said for Maureen, I walked in to see her. We were alone. She was resting peacefully. It occurred to me that the end was near. I sat next to her, and I grabbed her hand, which was very limp. With tears streaming down my face, I whispered in her ear, "Maureen, I promise I'll take good care of Megan." I don't know if she heard me, but I'm fairly certain that she did. I noticed a slight smile on her face, and her hand moved. It was all I could choke out. I couldn't talk. I was sobbing. I never had the strength to have "the discussion" with her about Megan, but at least she had my promise.

Later in the evening, Maureen developed some breathing problems, and the hospice nurse administered a shot to help her breathe more smoothly. Mom continued to lead us in the rosary throughout the evening.

When we put Megan to bed that evening, Jeri explained to her that the situation was grave. She asked Megan if she would like to be awakened during the night if Maureen was dying. She meekly replied that she wanted us to wake her up. We put Megan to bed around nine p.m. At ten-thirty p.m., Mom, Margie, and I also went to bed. Jeri informed us that Maureen could pass within hours in her condition. If there were changes, she would wake us up. She stayed in the spare bed, in the room, with Maureen. I marveled at Jeri and developed a new admiration for her. I knew she must be an exceptional nurse; her kindness and compassion were something to behold.

I literally crawled up the steps and got into bed with Megan on the pull-out sofa. Mom was in Megan's bed. I numbly said my prayers and surprisingly, fell right to sleep. A short time later, I was wrestled awake by Jeri. "Come downstairs, now!" I ran down the stairs and walked into the room to find Jack weeping at Maureen's bedside. *Oh, God! Please, no! No! No! This can't be really happening again. Please, someone, wake me up from the never-ending nightmare.* But it was no nightmare, and she was gone from us, our dearly beloved sister, our friend, our everything! Margie and I held each other up. We wept, dried our tears, and wept some more as I vaguely recalled walking up the stairs to awaken Mom. She came downstairs, and my eighty-four–year-old mother kissed her daughter goodbye. We numbly composed ourselves and prepared for the most heart-wrenching experience of our lives as Jeri gathered little Megan in her arms. She held her as Megan bent over to place a final kiss on her mother's cheek. All of us were reeling with grief. We remained with Maureen as this scene repeated itself again and again as other family members came to say their goodbyes.

The medical examiner arrived and pronounced Maureen legally dead on May first, 1995. The funeral home came and removed the body at approximately two a.m. We all sat in the living room as Maureen left her house for the last time.

After two or three hours of rest, we were up making calls. We called all our cousins in Ireland and all of our other relatives in Michigan. We called our employers and all of our friends. The nightmare was over. Maureen's suffering had ended. We had no doubt that she was in heaven. But now, how, in God's name, could we go on without her lilting laughter, her wonderful sense of humor, the beauty and grace she so generously shared with us? She was leaving a huge hole in all our hearts, and we knew our lives would never be the same.

After all the calls were made and a meager breakfast eaten, Megan woke up. We took her aside to explain that the funeral home representatives had come during the night to take her mom to the funeral home to prepare her for burial. She remembered and said very little. There was also very little emotional response. She did not cry.

Later that day, I decided it was time for me to go home. I had to spend one last day with my family as I knew it and prepare the way for Megan. Mom, Margie, and Jeri would take good care of Megan until the following day.

Since Margie had driven me to Maureen's house, I decided to drive Maureen's van to Lansing and return with it the following day for the visitation. I was only a few miles from her house when I noticed a Mary Chapin Carpenter cassette in her car. Margie, Maureen, and I often listened to her music because it reminded us of our relationship to each other and growing up together. I popped the cassette in the player but before too long, I found myself getting choked up. Instead of removing the tape, I left it in, and soon, I was sobbing. I pulled over, stopped the car, and found myself crying uncontrollably. I couldn't believe she was really gone. Why? How could I go on without her guidance and support and, most importantly, the love she'd given to me my entire life? How could I possibly take care of Megan when I felt like I couldn't even function? I don't know how long I stayed on the side of the road. I got out of the car, got some fresh air and continued to weep for a long time. It was the thought of home that caused me to regain my composure. I would find comfort there.

As I was coming into Lansing, driving on the expressway, an interesting event occurred. I was driving in the right lane and noticed a slower-moving vehicle in front of me. I pulled in the left-hand lane to pass the car, and just as I reached the point where I was probably in their blind spot, it was almost as if someone else took control of my van and pulled it onto the median. At the same instant, the car I was passing apparently decided it was going to pass the car in front of it. The driver pulled out, without noticing me, and would have surely hit me. I sat there disbelieving what had just happened, and I was reminded of Maureen's promise that she would never leave me. Again, I sat on the side of the road for a few minutes and tried to regain my composure before continuing my journey home.

It was great to be home. We spent a quiet evening together and talked to Matthew about the fact that Megan would be coming home with us and would become a part of our family. He was excited and had many things he wanted to share with her. We also worked on a photo board that we would take to the funeral home. I crawled into bed that evening and tried to focus on the moment. I wrapped myself in Mark's loving arms and, for the time being, felt safe. I didn't want to think about tomorrow and the next day. It was just too sad.

We awoke and prepared for the visitation later that afternoon. It was May second. The entire family gathered at the funeral home an hour before we accepted visitors. When I walked in and saw Maureen, I was shocked. I didn't even recognize her. It was almost as if she was someone else. It was probably difficult to disguise how the disease had ravaged her. I held onto my brother Tom and cried. From that point onward, I chose instead to focus on the picture boards signifying what had been ... and the wonderful times we had spent together.

One of the visitors that afternoon was Megan's first grade teacher from St. Patrick's Elementary School. She and her class had assembled a book for Megan. Each student had designed his or her own page expressing their sympathies in typical first grade fashion. It was priceless, and Megan still treasures it today. Many of my friends from school came that evening too, including my principal, Emily.

Margie and I had already discussed the many options that were offered concerning Megan's immediate care. Friends of Maureen's had offered to let Megan live with them until the end of the school year to allow her to finish the year in her school. It seemed tragic enough that she had lost her dad and mom. In two days she would be saying goodbye to her home. Was it necessary for her to lose her school and her friends as well?

Margie, with her psychological wisdom, determined that it was necessary. The transition would be much worse later. If she grew attached to her "foster" family, Megan would face yet another loss and sense of detachment. Therefore, the issue of finding a school in which Megan could finish the year was an immediate concern and weighed heavily on my mind.

I took Emily aside and asked if she could gain approval for me to bring Megan to school with me to finish her first grade year. This was prior to the "schools of choice" option in Michigan which allowed a child to attend a neighboring school if there were openings. Emily said it was perfectly fine with her and that she'd place Megan in Janet Peters' class, one of our first-grade teachers. She would seek the superintendent's approval first and let me know the following day. I felt a great sense of relief already, knowing that I would probably be able to take Megan to school with me every day.

We had booked a hotel in the Detroit area because the visitations would run late. We went back to the hotel, let the kids swim, and went to bed. The following day we had a leisurely morning. We went back to the funeral home later in the afternoon. That evening two of Maureen's best friends did eulogies for her. Dennis Hertel spoke about her great love for people and how she was such a great advocate for the "plain, ordinary citizen." She worked tirelessly on their behalf. He also mentioned that Maureen's sincerity and genuine concern for others were evident even to those who knew her for only a short time.

Milt Mack spoke second and relayed the humorous story of Maureen's piano playing. There were two things that were remarkable about the story. First, it was amazing that Maureen even had a piano. Mom and Dad must have saved every penny they had. Maureen was probably only seven or eight years old when they bought it for her. Many of us ended up taking lessons on the prized piano, but it was, clearly, Maureen's piano. Milt wove a story about the many times he had moved Maureen's piano. During college and beyond, she lived in many apartments, some of them on the second floor. Milt and a couple of his buddies would come to her rescue and move the piano for her ... up the stairs, down the stairs, around narrow corners, and into waiting trucks. They repeated the process every time she moved. He ended the tale with "You know, I never did see her play the damn thing!" Everyone laughed. It was so like Maureen. She could talk anyone into anything. Your reward, most of the time, was that you were lucky enough to know Maureen. You didn't need anything else. She was just so incredibly entertaining without intending to be so!

At some point during that evening, Megan was sitting with her cousins and at a more serious moment, burst out laughing. I approached her and told her she needed to settle down, or go downstairs if she wanted to play and have fun. She looked up at me and started crying, and like me on the side of the road, before long, she was sobbing. She was weeping ... almost hyper-ventilating, she was crying so hard. I held her and was relieved. Her seven-year-old heart and mind had held it in long enough. I'm sure at the moment I corrected her, she was thinking, "I want my mom!" and when she realized that her mom couldn't come to her, she let loose. She was like a lost lamb in a big, frightening world. I still can't imagine the immensity of what it must have been like for her. She sobbed and sobbed. We all sobbed. Eventually, she was done crying, jumped down, and passed the rest of the evening with her friends and cousins. Later, we went back to the hotel and tried to prepare for the funeral of Maureen the following day.

The funeral was held at St. Patrick's Church, which was next to Megan's school. Brother Ed sang at the funeral, and bag pipes played as we entered and exited. Midway through the funeral, one of Maureen and Dick's dearest friends, Roger, developed heart problems. Fortunately, Jeri and her husband, Chris, a firefighter, attended to him immediately. The service was momentarily stopped, his shirt was opened, and CPR began. An ambulance was called, and he was taken to the hospital. I thought the whole incident was ironic because his condition was symbolic of how we all felt. Every person in that church was suffering from a broken heart. Roger felt it in a very real way. Fortunately, Roger recovered and is doing fine.

Maureen's Eulogy

I don't remember a whole lot about the ceremony. I was consumed by grief. Maureen's close friend, and co-worker, Cathleen, gave the eulogy. She was kind enough to send me a copy a month or so after the funeral. I have reprinted it here:

"Like many of you, I have spent much time with Maureen during her illness, especially the past few weeks. And during that time, I cried much and learned much. I even laughed much, which shouldn't come as a surprise to those who knew Maureen. She was always smiling. Always.

"Also during this time, I had intense moments of spirituality. I'd like to tell you about those moments now. In the past week or so, I have learned more about cancer than I care to know. One terrible thing I learned was that patients like Maureen, as their illness worsens, come to experience episodes where their breathing stops—sometimes ten, fifteen, or even twenty seconds will pass with no breath. It's a terrible, frightening thing to witness. This happened to Maureen.

"Those of us who visited her during the final days shared in the privilege of keeping a vigil next to her bed so that she was never alone. During each of these precious moments when I was at her bedside, I often sat on the edge of my seat, realizing her breathing had stopped.

I would watch her chest, waiting and praying for it to rise again with a breath. And it did—every time I was there—it did.

"Quite often, when she would inhale, her eyes would flutter open and she would stare right back at me. I'm sure the expression on my face probably wasn't the most comforting thing! In fact, I thought about how it would drive me crazy to have someone watching me constantly, though I knew she did not want to be alone. So, I got up and went to her bookshelf and searched for something to read while I sat next to her. That way, I could still listen for her breathing.

"As you can imagine, Maureen's shelf was filled with books on government and politics, and a few on cancer. Finally, on the top shelf, I saw a book of poetry, which I took with me and returned to her bedside. When I opened it, it fell naturally to a page toward the middle of the book, and I remember thinking that this poem must be well-read for the book to open so naturally to it. This is that poem:

"Remember"
By Christina Rossetti

Remember me when I am gone away,
Gone far away into the silent land;
When you can no more hold me by the hand,
Nor I half turn to go, yet turning, stay.

Remember me when no more day by day
You tell me of our future that you planned;
Only remember me; you understand
It will be too late to counsel then or pray.

Yet if you should forget me for awhile
And afterwards remember, do not grieve;
For if the darkness and corruption leave
A vestige of the thoughts that once I had,
Better by far you should forget and smile
Than you should remember and be sad.

"I believe with all my heart that Maureen found a message in this poem, and I think that message is for all of us here, especially those who hurt for her the most, her family and her close, close friends.

"The message is one that Maureen lived. It is a message of life. No one ever lived life more fully than Maureen. She enjoyed life; she loved life. She would want each of you to pick up your lives again and to close the door on this terrible, terrible thing that has befallen her. She would rather that you smiled and forgot, rather than you remembered and grieved.

"Maureen does not need our prayers now.

"Rather, now my prayers go out to you, her family and friends. I pray that your lives will begin again and that you will be all the better for having known and loved Maureen, despite this cloud of sadness that is with us now."

As we exited the church and watched as Maureen was loaded into the hearse, I clung to my husband and brother, Tom. Maureen was driven away to be cremated. We went back into the parish hall for a luncheon. We were really not in the mood for food, but the companionship of our friends sustained us. We could feel their warmth and concern. Somehow, we had to continue our lives.

We left the church to attend to immediate needs. Mark and Leslie, our good friends, volunteered to fill their van with Megan's things and unload it at our house in Lansing. My husband also had our van, which we loaded up with Megan's things as well. Matt rode back to Lansing with Mark; I stayed back with Margie, Megan, and Mom to take care of some last-minute tasks at the house. When we finally had Margie's Jeep packed, Megan noticed that her cat, Squirt, was sitting in the driveway. She asked me if we could take Squirt with us. Even though I had an elderly Irish setter at home, how could I say "No"? Here was a child who had lost everything near and dear to her. She had lost her mom and dad, her friends, her school, her house, her very life as she knew it, when we closed the door for the last time. So, Squirt rode on my lap to Lansing. He had basically been a barn cat, which would have to change. We lived in the middle of the city. He would have to become an inside cat.

This, by far, was one of the darkest days of my life. I had just said my final good-bye to my dear sister and was delivering a devastated child to a new, strange home. What could I possibly offer her? I was overwhelmed with feelings of inadequacy. I began to pray and have another discussion with God, even though I was extremely angry at him. I would deal with the "whys" of all this someday. I would hold Him accountable. Why couldn't a little miracle have taken place here? Surely, we deserved one. We were good people. Maureen was my angel sister. *Why* did she have to die?

I continued to think similar thoughts for some time. Eventually, it became apparent to me that it was not my will, but His that would be done. I was His instrument. He would have to help Mark and me, as would Maureen and Dick, and the rest of my family. As for Megan, the answer was pretty clear: *just love her!* In every sense, this would become a labor of love. In some ways, I had always felt like Megan's second mom. I was her godmother. She would often prefer me over others when she was fussy as an infant. As she got older, she would prefer to be with us because Matthew was her cousin and her friend. It was a blessing that Maureen and I were so close and had spent so much time together. It would make the transition easier for Megan. Megan was also close to her cousin, Maggie. She was like another older sister to her. I also knew that the rest of the family would also provide support and love.

We arrived in Lansing, opened the door of the car, and Squirt jumped out of my lap and bolted underneath the car. He was very confused, had just completed his first car ride, and had no idea where he was. Needless to say, he had another big surprise waiting: our Irish setter was inside the house eagerly waiting to greet him.

The four of us spent the weekend alone. We had business to attend to—the business of creating a new family. We packed up some of Matthew's toys to make room for Megan's Barbie's and play kitchen in our basement play room. Matthew approved, because we were only moving a few of his toys to the attic. We transformed our guest room into Megan's bedroom. It would be years, however, before she would sleep in it. She preferred the company of Matthew, so we bought her "girly" bedding for the top bunk. They would spend countless hours each night, talking and bonding. In retrospect, it was a very good arrangement for both of them, because they needed each other. It provided additional security, above and beyond what Mark and I could offer to them. I was in no hurry for her to sleep in her room. I knew she would let me know when she was ready.

With the exception of Megan, we all returned to our former lives on Monday. Mark went to work, Matt went to his school, I went to my school, and Megan came with me to her new school. As we drove the half-hour drive to school that morning, she did not appear to be nervous. I told her I would take her to her new classroom and stay with her as long as she needed me. She very bravely walked into the class with me, met Mrs. Peters, her new teacher, and announced that she would be fine. I explained that I would be right down the hall, and left her there. We had lunch together at McDonald's, and I took her back to school for the afternoon. This process was repeated every day until school was out for the year, the second week in June.

In spite of the fact that Megan was in Mrs. Peters' classroom for only a month, she completely changed the dynamics of that classroom. It was inevitable that the kids would eventually find out "Megan's story." The way in which they learned her story was even more remarkable. Many of the kids began to ask questions about why Megan was with me. Was I her mommy? Where did she live? Why was she with me? Megan decided she would just tell them. So, when she was "star of the week", she stood up in front of her new classmates and told them what had happened in her life. You can imagine how the other little first-graders reacted. At first, it was beyond their comprehension. They went home and told their parents about their new classmate whose *mom and dad* had died. Parents called the teacher for verification, believing that it was a typical first-grade fabrication.

In the end, Megan changed the lives of those first-graders. They hugged more, loved more, laughed more, and learned to value every minute of life. They learned at a very young age not to take things for granted. Years later, the teachers in the middle school would talk about how particularly empathetic a certain group of students were, and they traced the kids back to Mrs. Peters class of which Megan became a part during that last month of school in May of 1995.

Within the time frame of thirty months, I had experienced the deaths of three significant people in my life. I knew that I had only one choice. Looking back and reflecting on what I had lost would worsen my devastation. I had to allow myself time to grieve, and at the same time, I had to force myself to look ahead. I was ready to begin a new life, with a new family.

Maureen McGlinchey DeShetler & Richard DeShetler

New Beginnings

Changes

We were all very happy when school was out for the summer. We had a garage sale at the beginning of the summer to continue to "make room for Megan." Our main problem was that we had only one bathroom in our house. Although it was possible for all four of us to get showered in the morning, it was not very pleasant. Our house was built in 1927 and also had very little closet space. We loved our house and our neighbors, but we had to consider moving. We looked at many houses, none of which impressed us. We began to look at option two. We never sold our first house, which was around the corner from our present home. We decided we would sell the rental house and put an addition onto our current house. We added an upstairs room above the back porch and a bathroom above the first-floor breakfast nook. It gave Megan her own closet and a bathroom for the kids. The house was perfect for everyone.

Another immediate problem was a school for Megan. Maureen and Dick had stated in the will that they wanted her Catholic education to continue. I visited many Catholic schools in Lansing and settled on St. Therese, in north Lansing. It would be her fourth school in two years. She had attended a Young Fives program and kindergarten in the public school, and attended first grade at both St. Patrick's and Union Street. She was becoming an expert at being the "new student."

St. Therese seemed to be a good choice for us. Everyone there was loving and kind and took Megan under their wings. She met many wonderful friends who remain her very close friends to this day. Matthew had spent his kindergarten year in the neighborhood public school at the end of our street. He had a great teacher and a very successful year, but the thought of maintaining three different school schedules was a little overwhelming to us. Since we did not want to separate Megan and Matthew, we enrolled Matthew at St. Therese as well.

I continued to sing in the choir every Sunday, and Matthew and Megan would sit in the loft with me. I was mostly just "going through the motions." Spiritually, I was numb. I remained angry with God. I suppose in some sense, I was going through the stages of grief. At first, I was relieved that Maureen was no longer suffering. Then I was angry that she ever had to suffer in the first place. I believe in miracles. Why couldn't Maureen have been the recipient of one?

In order to help me adjust to life without Maureen and Dick, I talked to them all the time and knew they were helping me with the many decisions that had to be made. While I was visiting the various schools, I asked them to guide my decision and help me to find the best place for Megan. On the day I visited St. Therese, the principal, Tom, was outside with the kids for field day. I had just left another Catholic school on the west side of Lansing and was told there were no openings. The principal, however, asked me if I had considered St. Therese. I told her I hadn't, and she explained that it should definitely be an option. She proceeded to call St. Therese and informed them that she was sending me over to them. When I arrived, I was greeted warmly by the secretary, who immediately called Tom on a walkie-talkie. He came off the playground, sat with me for a long time, explained the program at St. Therese, and assured me they would take care of both Megan and Matthew. He also introduced me to the teachers the kids would have in the fall. He gave me a tour of the building and walked me to my car. I sat out in the parking lot for a long time and felt that I was guided to this place for a reason. This would be their school. I felt that Maureen and Dick had a hand in sending me to St. Therese.

Megan and Matthew seemed to flourish in their new surroundings. Megan had a great teacher, and she continued to be a very good student. The same was true for Matthew. I was teaching full-time in Eaton Rapids. Mark would drop the kids off in the morning before he went to work. After school, they went to a multicultural after-school program to learn conversational Spanish. My friend, Juanita, who sang in the choir with me, was the director of the program. I knew her personally and had no doubts that she would take good care of both of them.

In September, Maureen and Dick's house sold. We had left the house after her funeral and had not returned since. It was time to go back and say goodbye for the last time. Cleaning out the house was a very difficult task. Although Maureen and Dick had specified where the big items should go, there was still a houseful of things that had to be removed. We set a date to go and move the contents out of the house. Everyone was there, including Megan and Matt. Margie and I got the task of cleaning up Maureen and Dick's bedroom. As we were going through Maureen's drawers, we found two cards addressed to Megan. They were not sealed, so we read them. They were amazing. In each, Maureen explained how much she loved Megan. In the first, she had just been diagnosed and explained to Megan how she was going to fight to win her breast cancer battle. The second was written much later, when she knew she was losing the battle. In it, she explained that if she didn't make it, Mark and I would be her new "mom and dad." Amazingly, she used the opportunity to give Megan advice about how she should live her life. Without quoting her exactly, it was worded something like this: *During your life, you should make "doing the right thing" your guiding principle. If you do that, you will know happiness beyond measure.* It was a perfect description of Maureen. We were both sobbing as we read the notes. We showed them to Jeri and Liz, and they, too, were amazed. I didn't show them to Megan that day. I put them away and showed them to her years later, when she could fully understand the enormity of the messages.

We continued to clean out the house. It took pretty much the entire weekend. Maureen and Dick's wrap-around porch was filled with items for Purple Heart, a charitable organization. I took home very few items: Maureen's red winter dress coat, a few other items of clothing, and Dick's old desk that had been in their bedroom. I couldn't get out of the house fast enough. How could a place that had brought us such joy and had entertained so many people have turned into a place of such sadness? I wanted to set off a bomb in the room where they had both died. I was obviously still mourning and still angry.

Before we left, we took some pictures outside and said our final goodbyes to the old place. Megan walked around on the grounds, visited the barn and her "climbing tree," and said her goodbyes in her own way. It was the only house she had ever known. My heart was breaking for her. Ironically, it was not the last time we visited the house.

A Healing Place

After Maureen died, I continued to remain in contact with Ele's Place, a center in Lansing for grieving children and their families. They provided useful information concerning Megan's care and some basic information about the grieving process. Unfortunately, the center had a waiting list, and we wouldn't be able to attend their sessions until September. Finally, we were contacted, and we attended Ele's Place every Wednesday night for almost a year. While there, the schedule involved attending sessions, sharing a meal, and grieving together. Matthew and Megan were in separate sessions. Mark and I were together with the adults. When I inquired why Megan and Matthew couldn't be in the same sessions together, their response made sense. Their grief would be very different. Megan, obviously, would be grieving for her parents and her former life. Matthew would be grieving for his godparents and his former life, as well. But he might be afraid to truly express his feeling while Megan was present, and vice-versa.

Each week, the adults, too, had their own session. We were seated in a circle in a separate room, and I clearly remember the first night. The leaders asked us to go around the circle, introduce ourselves, and state why we were at Ele's Place. When it was my turn, I had just started to tell about Dick and realized I couldn't finish. I got too choked up and started to cry. Thankfully, Mark finished the story. Everyone was very sympathetic and supportive.

Ele's Place was truly a "healing place." We met many great people who remain our friends. There were many nights when we would drag ourselves there, but on the way home, we were always thankful that we had attended. Gradually, as the year went on, we came to the realization that Ele's Place had done their job. We would always grieve for those former days and our former lives with our loved ones. Somehow, however, the grief didn't seem to hurt as much. The horror of Dick and Maureen's deaths was gradually being replaced with sweet memories. The most important thing we learned at Ele's Place was that there is no timeline for grief. We would never feel completely "normal" again. Instead, we would feel "normal" most of the time, but there would always be that place in our hearts and at our tables where someone was missing.

Christmas

The fall passed quickly, and before we knew it, we had entered the Christmas season. As I stated earlier, there were many times when I could almost sense the presence of Maureen and Dick when it came to Megan's care. It gives me chills to think about our first Christmas together. We had decorated the house, and it was time to set up the Christmas tree. We went out together to cut one down, brought it home, and set it up. Mark helped get the decorations out of the attic; we put on some Christmas music and proceeded to decorate the tree. We had put only a few decorations on the tree when I noticed that Megan had disappeared. At the time, the kids had their playroom down in the basement. I went down there and asked Megan why she didn't want to help decorate the tree. She replied very simply and honestly, "None of those decorations are mine." It's difficult for me to express how foolish and inept I felt. Why hadn't I thought of this beforehand? How could I have been so damned insensitive? I apologized to her profusely and assured her that we would make it better.

The very next morning, I got up to do our usual Saturday chores. Later in the afternoon, when the mail was delivered, I noticed that there was a little package for Megan. I called her to come and open it. As she opened it and the contents became visible, I am at a loss for words to describe how I felt. Inside was a beautifully crossed-stitched Christmas ornament with Megan's name on it. I remembered Maureen's promise that she would never leave me. I had a profound sense that both Maureen and Dick were standing beside me at that moment. It was almost like they were saying, "It's okay ... when you don't think of something, we'll fill in the gaps." The story behind the ornament is a simple one. The parishioners at St. Therese were presented with a basket in the fall with all the names of the second-graders that would be making their First Communion in the spring. Megan's communion sponsor had made the ornament for her. It was just so overwhelming that we received it on the morning following our tree-decoration "disaster."

To make amends, I quickly got on the phone and talked to Jeri and Jill about Maureen's Christmas ornaments. Eventually, they were found, I received them, and we kept all of Megan's special decorations. The most priceless one has a recording of Dick on his last Christmas. You push a button, and he says, "Merry Christmas, Megan. I love you."

School, Irish Step Dancing and Adoption

During the first few months after Megan became a part of our family, I started looking for a place for her to continue her Irish step dancing lessons. I was reluctantly going to drive her down to her old school, which was about an hour and a half from Lansing. Fortunately, however, there was a group that was just beginning to form in Lansing with John Heinzman from Detroit as the instructor. I quickly enrolled her, and when Matthew piped up and said he would like to try it, I enrolled him as well. Before long, they were jumping, jigging, and reeling all around the house. It was great to watch them. Whenever Mom would come up to Michigan for the summer, she loved to go to their shows and lessons to watch them dance. It turned out that the dancing and the music were very therapeutic for all of us. It brought back some of those sweet memories, as well as being a big part of our heritage. Many of the kids who danced also played the violin, and Megan became fascinated with the instrument. She expressed an interest in learning to play, and so we enrolled her at Michigan State University's Community Music School. The violin, as well as dancing, became Megan's favorite activities.

During the first year after Maureen's death, I often contemplated Megan's future. Could she survive the death of her parents without severe emotional problems? I prayed and prayed that she would remain resilient and strong. Then, one Saturday, we were at home, just "chillin'." The stereo was playing in the living room, and I was in the kitchen. I heard boisterous laughter and walked into the living room to find Megan in the arms of Mark. He was spinning her around to the music, and she had the most joyful look on her face. I was struck at that moment by two things: First, perhaps Megan *would* be okay. Perhaps we would all be okay. Secondly, I reflected on my husband. At that moment, I fell in love with him all over again. To me, he was the epitome of a man. I considered all that he had compassionately tolerated in the last year. Many men would have walked out the door and never looked back. Mark had the strength and courage to talk to Maureen when I couldn't. He comforted all of us when we needed it. It was clear to me that I had chosen a real gem for my husband.

Megan's second-grade year went by very quickly. She did very well in school and had many good friends. When she was in third grade, the school hired a new principal. I remember she called me one morning in late fall and asked if I could attend a parent meeting the following week around eight-thirty in the morning. I responded that I would just have to make some adjustments in my own schedule at school, but I would be there. She stated the meeting would take place in the church.

When I arrived at the church on November 4, 1996, I noticed that there was only one other parent in the church. I sat for awhile and soon noticed the students filing into the church. I began to wonder what kind of meeting we were going to have. Before long, the principal stood up and explained that we had gathered to honor two students in the building. She talked at length about each. When she began to talk about Megan, I remember clearly what she said. She explained that very rarely in our lives, we might be lucky enough to meet someone who is a model for all of us. In spite of great trouble and hardship, they have a smile on their face each day and prefer to count their blessings rather than dwell on negative events in their lives. As I was listening to the principal in the back of the church, I began to comprehend why I was there. The "meeting" was actually disguised as an opportunity to award Megan. The sweetness and magnitude of the event finally registered with me, and I began crying. She finished her accolades of Megan and asked me to come up to the front of the church. We have a great picture of the teacher, principal, Megan, and me standing behind an "A+ Achievement" banner. I was so proud of Megan and all that she had accomplished. There was no doubt that she was loved and, in her small way, was also touching the many lives of the people with whom she came in contact. It was another indication that Megan was, indeed, going to be "okay".

After Megan joined our family, Mark and I began formal proceedings to adopt her. We had been through the process with Matthew, but this time, it was different. First, we had to become legal guardians. We were co-guardians for more than a year while we filed the papers for the adoption. We had to make many appearances in front of the judge as we went through each stage of the process. Finally, on April 15, 1997, we were scheduled to go in front of the judge for the last time and make the adoption official. We invited family, friends, and our neighbors to join us in the courtroom. There were probably fifty people who crowded into the courtroom that day. It was a very emotional day for me. I remember the judge asking Mark and me some formal questions about Megan and how things were going. He addressed the people in the courtroom and thanked them for coming.

Finally, he spoke to Megan for a minute and pronounced her a "very lucky little girl." I remember thinking at the time, how in God's holy name could she be "lucky"? Her parents were dead! Later, however, I began to look at things from his perspective. I'm sure that during his time on the bench, he had seen many children who had no one to love or care for them. Worse yet, many of the children who came to his courtroom were probably horribly abused and lived in terrible conditions. Anyway, the judge finally banged the gavel, and Megan was legally our daughter. She chose to keep her DeShetler name, which was fine with both of us. After the court hearing, we had arranged to have an open house for

Megan. It was a beautiful spring day, and many people came to give her presents and offer their best wishes. Many of Maureen and Dick's former neighbors and friends came, which was great for Megan. We tried to make the day as special as we could. Mark and I now had a boy and a girl, both of whom were great gifts in every sense of the word.

Megan and Matt spent another year at St. Therese. At the end of Megan's fourth grade year, the school began to have financial difficulties. I was devastated to discover that the plan for the 1998-1999 academic year was to create a fourth-fifth grade split classroom, which would have meant that Matthew and Megan would be in the same classroom. I did not like that idea at all. Both Matthew and Megan still needed validation and separation in their new life. Although I had no doubt whatsoever that they truly cared about one another, spending twenty-four hours a day together would be a little too much closeness.

When it became apparent that the split classroom proposal was actually going to happen, I was, once again, shopping for a school. This time, my journey took me to the home of the Shamrocks, Resurrection School. The principal, who had also battled breast cancer, assured me that both Megan and Matthew would be well cared for in their new school. As it turned out, many other children from St. Therese transferred as well, so the kids had many former friends that joined them at Resurrection.

Resurrection was also a great school. Megan's fifth-grade class included a mixture of new girls and "Res" girls. We were delighted to discover that one of Megan's Ele's Place friends, Allison, was a student at Resurrection. Allison's mother had died of breast cancer too, so she and Megan had developed a special bond. Allison's father, Larry, had been in the adult sessions at Ele's Place, so we knew him as well. Coincidentally, he was also the fifth-grade girl's basketball coach. Basketball was a very popular sport at Resurrection, and it seemed as if every fifth-grade girl was on the team. Two or three weeks of the season had already passed when a group of the girls approached Larry and told them about Megan.

They wanted her to be able to join the basketball team. Megan had never really played basketball, but they were determined to have her on the team. She eventually joined them and played basketball with them until she left Resurrection after the eighth grade. Larry took her under his wing, as did so many loving people.

Matthew and Megan had very good teachers at Resurrection. They all took a sincere interest not only in their academics, but in their lives. They would take the kids out to lunch or to dinners in the evening. Megan and Matt always enjoyed helping their teachers, so I'm sure the teachers were repaying them for their help. It demonstrated, however, that the teachers enjoyed spending their personal time with the kids. I was always thankful for their special kindness.

During the summer of 1999, we were very happy to be able to visit Ireland. Fortunately, Mark and I had been able to visit on numerous occasions before this, but the kids had never been there. In addition, my mother had dropped many hints, in a not-so-subtle manner that she wished to return home to visit Ireland. She was quite clever. She began a lobbying campaign by dropping hints that she would like to get to Ireland "one more time before I die to see my dear sister, Nellie." It's pretty difficult to say no when a request is worded in such a manner. We all began to feel pretty guilty and worked to make her visit happen. She was eighty-nine at the time, but still in pretty good shape.

On August thirteenth, Mark, Megan, Matt, Mom, and I boarded a plane and flew to Ireland. We had a glorious time. We visited my cousins in Woodford and Mount Shannon. Mom was able to visit Nellie, and she took many side trips with us. On August 21, the town of Mount Shannon hosted a fair or festival, and my cousin asked if Megan and Matt would dance for it. They agreed. It was really quite humorous. A sheet of plywood was thrown on the street, the music started playing, and their feet started flying. Soon, a crowd gathered around them, and you could hear the comments: "Look at the Yanks dance!" or "Hurry, come and see the two Yanks dancing!" It was great fun. During the rest of the trip, we visited many different beautiful locations in Ireland and tried to show the kids as much of the country as possible.

Matthew and Megan continued to take Irish step dancing lessons, and each year, they would participate in the talent show at Resurrection. They chose the music and choreographed their own dances. The staff and kids loved to watch them dance.

Eventually, The Irish Dance Company of Lansing formed as a splinter group from the traditional weekly lesson group. The new group would provide the kids with the opportunity to perform in venues other than the traditional Irish Feis competitions. There were approximately twenty dancers in the group, and they varied in age from five to eighteen. They performed all over the state for different functions. It was fun to drive them around and take part in many of the Irish festivals, St. Patrick's Day parties, and many other events. They danced all year, not only during March. This "traveling troupe" gave Megan and Matthew the opportunity to meet new friends from other schools and other towns. They had parties and sleepovers, and an added charm was that Mark and I also met many new parent-friends. I know that Dick and Maureen were smiling down on Megan every time she danced. Watching Megan do a slip jig would always bring tears to my eyes. It's a slow, beautiful dance performed only by girls, and Megan could do an amazing slip jig.

The Old House

That summer, we ventured back to Milford for the graduation of Megan's dear friend, Johnny. Sue and Pete, Maureen and Dick's neighbors and very dear friends, were having an Open House. Johnny was their youngest, and Megan and he were good buddies, along with her other childhood neighborhood friend, "Glenny." They had a little tree just beyond the house which they named the "climbing tree." They would meet there often and climb the tree and have many childhood conversations. We had heard that Maureen and Dick's house had been re-sold and the new owners were very friendly. One day, Jeri decided to pay them a visit, informed them that she had once lived in the house, and was welcomed with open arms. The owner said to let everyone know they would be welcomed if anyone wanted to visit the "old place."

After we left the open house, we decided to stop by and see if anyone was home. As we pulled in the driveway, we noticed the man of the house out in the yard, working. He approached the car, we told him who we were, and he said, "Oh, my gosh! My wife is inside. She would love to meet you." As we walked up the very familiar steps and approached the door, we were greeted with an Irish "Welcome" sign. We were given a tour of the house, which had been changed considerably, yet it was still very familiar. The most surprising part of our visit was learning that the new family was very Irish. The daughter took Irish step dancing lessons and had an Irish step dancing doll, identical to Megan's, which was proudly displayed in the dining room. The house presented itself with the same good, family presence that it had when Maureen and Dick were there.

I left the house with a very different feeling than I had in September, 1995, when we moved all of Maureen and Dick's possessions out of the house. The house, once again, had become a place of joy. A new family was making new memories, and I'm sure a new little girl was Irish step dancing for her parents in the same room where Megan had danced for her mom and dad. The irony was amazing, and I always thought that perhaps Maureen and Dick had a hand in the way things turned out with regards to their great home.

High School Years and Beyond

Unbelievably, in June of 2002, we attended Megan's graduation from eighth grade. She received many awards and honors and would be heading off to Lansing Catholic High School in the fall. I felt a great sense of accomplishment for her. It was clear to me that she had made some deliberate choices in her life. Instead of focusing on the things she didn't have, she placed her focus on her blessings. She, of all people, had the right to be angry at the cards she had been dealt in life. She had plenty of reasons to choose the "wrong path." Instead, I'm convinced that she has become a model for others. The tragedy in her life would be hard to surpass. She knew more about grief and dying as a child than most adults experience in a lifetime. She was an expert. I know that she used her experiences to help others when they lost loved ones. She remains an inspiration to me in so many ways.

Many people have also commented, without knowing Megan's life circumstances, that she is such a positive person and never seems to have a bad day. Like her mother, she always has a smile on her face. Without speaking for her, I think I know why. Megan knows, firsthand, how to define a bad day. It was a bad day when she had to kiss her dad goodbye for the last time. It was a bad day when she had to kiss her mom goodbye for the last time. Every other day, in comparison, has to be a defined as a good day.

Megan began high school in the fall of 2002. She had tried out for cheerleading during the summer and became a member of the cheerleading squad. She loved it. I had not really attended any of their practices and was excited to go to their first game. I was totally ignorant as to the changes that had occurred in cheerleading since I was in high school. It turns out that Megan was a "flyer." I nearly fainted at that first game when they threw her up in the air. She has always been an adventuresome type, just like her father. She loved it…and the higher, the better. I gradually adjusted to her "flying," but there were many prayers involved. Thankfully, she was never totally dropped. She injured her ankle when she landed incorrectly after a jump, and that was the extent of her injuries. It seemed like the bases, the girls that "catch" her, were injured more often than Megan.

Megan thrived academically at Lansing Catholic. She took mostly honors classes and maintained a very high grade point average. It was a great school for both Megan and Matt. The teachers were kind and considerate, as well as being very competent. "Father Joe" was also there full time. He's a young priest, drives a pickup truck, and is very "cool." The student body loves him and he is a great role model. Both Megan and Matt thought very highly of him. He attended most of the sporting events at the school and was always on the sidelines at the football games. I remember one evening, at an unusually warm football game, he dug into the cooler with water bottles in it and started passing them out to the cheerleaders. I was so impressed. He was also very supportive at their competitions, as was Jenny, the athletic director. Once again, it was great that the kids were supported and surrounded by caring people.

Unlike many parents, Mark and I enjoyed the teenaged years. Matthew and Megan never became defiant or uncontrollable. Of course, you hear and read horror stories of some teenagers who are always "testing the waters." Both kids were very busy in high school. They didn't have time to explore "other options," or make "bad choices." Megan's dance, cheerleading and violin lessons kept her busy. Matt was interested in drama, so the drama productions, dance and voice lessons kept him busy. Most importantly, they chose good friends. All of the friends they brought to our house were great kids. As they got older, being only a year apart, they had mutual friends and were also friends with one another. It has always been a source of comfort to me that they have each other.

I think most of the teachers at Lansing Catholic knew "Megan's story." Megan's cheerleading coach and teacher was a source of comfort and friendship to Megan throughout high school. In the fall of 2005, both the varsity and junior varsity cheerleading squads, which totaled approximately thirty girls, attended the "Making Strides Against Breast Cancer" race in downtown Lansing. It just so happened that the cheerleading squad that had been recruited to hold the ribbons for the breast cancer survivors to run through had failed to appear. Consequently, the Lansing Catholic cheerleaders were asked to hold the ribbons. In addition, the junior varsity coach presented Megan with a pink Breast Cancer Survivor shirt. She started crying, I started crying, and pretty soon, most of us were crying. I sought Megan out, and we hugged each other for a minute and then returned to the business at hand. As I began walking with my friend, Stephanie, however, I was again struck by the irony of the situation. Megan, in my eyes, exemplifies a true "survivor." Her mom may not have been able to survive breast cancer, but Megan will pick up where Maureen left off and make it possible for others to survive. We enjoyed the walk and completed it with the cheerleaders. Megan and I have participated in a number of cancer walks since then, and will continue to do so.

In another cancer fundraising event, our family sponsored a golf outing we called the "DeShetler Open." My nephew, Eddie, would make all the arrangements. Friends and family would come to the golf course to enjoy a game of golf, and then we would picnic afterwards with non-golfing friends and family. We raised thousands of dollars over the years for cancer research in memory of Maureen and Dick. It was an opportunity to get together with many of their old friends, most of whom we would not see otherwise. We have not held the outing during the past few years, but another of my nephews, Kevin, has begun a golf outing in late summer called "The Late Summer Classic." The proceeds go to the McCarty Cancer Foundation, and many of the people who attended the DeShetler Open now choose to golf in this outing. Kevin has managed to raise thousands of dollars for this foundation. The bottom line is that we are supporting cancer research in some small way and are having fun while we do it.

In Megan's junior year at Lansing Catholic, another memorable event took place. Every spring, at the end of the cheerleading season, a banquet takes place for all the cheerleaders and their parents. Each year, one athlete is given the St. Sebastian award. When it came time to give the award, Jenny, the athletic director, explained the history of the award. St. Sebastian is the patron saint of athletes and the award symbolizes "leadership and a positive attitude." Jenny explained that the recipient should exemplify these characteristics and many other positive attributes. Next, the cheerleading coach stood to talk about the recipient for the 2004-2005 school year. To be honest, I was only partially attentive, because the recipient is usually a senior. After a couple of minutes, however, I began to think that Jodi was describing Megan. She described how she, herself, had been touched by "this person." She also mentioned that the recipient had taught her many things about how to live, and to keep a positive attitude, in spite of "bad times." Slowly, I began to realize that Megan was going to receive the award, and like so many other times, I began to cry. Every time Megan is recognized for something, I can't help but think how proud Maureen and Dick would be and how much I wish they could see what a wonderful person she has grown to be. I wish I could celebrate such joys with them. Anyway, as I sat at the banquet in my emotional state, my friend, Stephanie had some good advice for me: "You better get ready for next year!"

Stephanie's advice was well-taken. There were many milestones as Megan completed her last year in high school. We had previously discussed the fact that this would be her year of "lasts." She would have her last "first day" of high school, her "last homecoming", her "last winter ball", etc. My advice to her was to treasure every moment and to have fun! Rather than taking lots of advanced placement classes, she remained in the typical college-bound honors classes because we didn't want a high stress level to be the defining memory of her senior year.

As graduation neared, I had mixed feelings. I didn't want Megan's high school years to end. I actually had fun following her to cheerleading competitions and going to football and basketball games. I met many wonderful people as a result of the activities in which Megan was involved. On the other hand, as she got ready to graduate, I also felt a huge sense of accomplishment. Mark and I had managed to raise Dick and Maureen's daughter with virtually no problems. My paralyzing fear as I drove home with her so many years ago after Maureen's funeral proved to be unfounded.

In the spring of Megan's senior year, my "discussions" with Maureen and Dick became more frequent. I told them that this accomplishment was not only about Mark and me. They needed to, once again, share in the joy of what was about to happen. They had created this wonderful child. I invited them to share in the celebrations that were about to occur, and they didn't disappoint me.

Two events in the spring of Megan's senior year were memorable in this regard. The first occurred at the "Father Mac" dinner, which is a fundraiser for scholarships to Lansing Catholic. Since it is a pricey event, I don't usually feel as though I can spend the money, but a featured speaker that year was Joe DeLamielleure, my friend from Centerline. He started his football career at St. Clement's, and we were in the same grade. We had grown up together. He also had a big, Catholic family, so for just about everyone in my family, there was a corresponding DeLamielleure who was a friend. I followed Joe's football career, including his induction into the National Football Hall of Fame. With great anticipation, I drove to the Father Mac dinner with my friend, Sandy, and Megan, who had volunteered to work at the event with other cheerleaders.

When we first arrived, we were assigned to a table, much like a wedding reception. We visited with the people at our table, none of whom I had ever met before. It was quite loud at the time, so it was difficult to catch the first and last names of everyone at our table. We visited for awhile and had dinner, and then I decided to go see Joe before he gave his speech. It was great to talk to him about the "old times" and growing up in Centerline. He ended up marrying Geri, a girl in our class and a friend of mine, so we talked about her as well. We had a wonderful visit, and I was struck by his sweetness. He was still the same Joe, a super-nice guy in every way. We hugged, and I returned to my seat before he gave his keynote address.

In the process of giving his speech, he talked about good ol' Centerline and what fun it was to grow up there. In particular, he mentioned St. Clement's and all the wonderful big, Catholic families that were quite common in that area. Then he said, "As a matter of fact, I can't believe that Kathleen McGlinchey is here." I thought that was very sweet, but then something else happened. The gentleman who was sitting immediately to my left said, "Oh my God, was Maureen your sister?" I responded affirmatively, and then he explained that he had worked with Maureen for years. He knew Dick as well and had attended their wedding. He also knew about their untimely deaths. He talked for awhile about how much he liked Maureen and loved her Irish wit and smile. I told Jim that Megan, their daughter, was at the event and asked if he and his wife would like to meet her. He said they would be thrilled.

I brought Megan over to them. I could see that he was very moved to meet her. He was literally shaking. After being introduced, he began to talk about how he loved Maureen and what a wonderful person she was. He got teary-eyed, and pretty soon, like so many times before, we were all crying *again*. I think Megan loved hearing about her mom from someone other than family. I felt the presence of Maureen that night. It was a wonderful evening.

The second event occurred shortly after the fundraising dinner. One day, Megan informed me that it was time to go prom shopping. I was struck by the fact that this would be her "last high school prom". We went to a number of shops but ended up at a shop that sells only prom and wedding attire. Before we went in, I informed Megan that I could not spend lots of money because Matt was going to the prom, also. When considering the price of a dress, tux, tickets, flowers, etc., it would be easy to spend well over five hundred dollars. Fortunately, Megan had been working at a Methodist church on Sunday mornings doing child care, and she said she would be willing to spend some of her money on the dress. It sounded like a good deal to me.

We entered the store, and she began to try on dresses. Megan has a tiny, petite build like her mother. She was not having much luck finding a dress until she found a white dress with coral roses trailing down the sides of it. When she tried it on and asked me to give her my opinion, I was stunned. I told her how beautiful she was, and how she reminded me so much of her mother. Then I said, "By the way, did I ever tell you that your mother was prom queen?"

She said, "No, that's really cool!" I proceeded to tell her about how I watched as Maureen got ready for her prom that evening. I wanted to grow up to be just like her, which was pretty much impossible. I was five feet, seven inches tall and a "string of misery," as my mother used to say in a joking fashion. But Maureen? She was a picture of beauty that night as she left for her senior prom.

Megan decided to buy the gorgeous dress and used two hundred dollars of her own money. I reminded her that it was her last prom and it was all about making memories, so it was money well spent.

On the Friday of the prom, the students were excused from school at noon. Megan had an appointment to get her hair done at 1:00. I had an in-service that day, so I was able to get home earlier than usual. When she walked in the house with her hair beautifully done, she said, "Guess what? I was nominated to be on the prom court today." At Lansing Catholic, the principal goes to each classroom in the morning and asks the students to vote for three girls and three boys to serve on the prom court. The results are announced at the end of the day. Then, at the prom, the kids vote for king and queen at the beginning of the evening.

After Megan told me she was on the court, the first thing out of my mouth was, "Oh my God, you're going to be prom queen."

She looked at me very strangely and said, "What are you talking about? I'm happy to be on the court. I don't care if I'm queen."

Of course, then I expressed how correct she was, and it was wonderful that she was chosen to be on the court. In the back of my mind, however, I couldn't help but think that Maureen was up to something. It was almost like she was saying, "If I was queen, then by golly, my daughter will be queen, too."

As Megan continued to get dressed that evening, she looked more beautiful with each passing moment. By the time her date arrived, she was as stunning as I remembered her mother being so many years ago. We took pictures of both of the kids at home, I followed Megan to her friend's house, and then I went to the location of the prom and shot some more pictures of the kids. The last thing I said to Megan before they closed the doors was, "Call me if you're elected queen." Again, she dismissed me, and away she went.

Mark and I went out to dinner and returned home for a very quiet evening by ourselves. I had gone upstairs and was watching television and reading a book. It must have been around 10:00 when the phone rang. It was Megan. She was crying, and only said, "Kathleen, I'm queen!" I couldn't speak; I was too busy crying. I waited up until she returned home. I caught her coming up the stairs. We just hugged, and I told her how happy I was for her. I also mentioned that I was quite convinced that her mother had been working on her behalf. She agreed. She stayed only for a little while before taking off for the "after prom" celebration at the YMCA. The next day, she told me all about the great time that she had the entire evening. It definitely fell into the category of a "making memories" event.

The author with Megan DeShetler.

Before long, graduation day arrived. Many family members attended, including Megan's half-siblings, Scott, Jeri, and Jill and their spouses. Jill had requested beforehand that we not inform Megan that she and her family would be flying in from Tennessee. Megan was very surprised to see them. The graduation ceremony was supposed to be a dignified event. The principal had told the graduating class ahead of time to keep things serious. He didn't want families to be loud and inappropriate. In our case, that was a pretty unrealistic expectation, especially when you consider the personalities of Megan's half-siblings. They are as fun loving as their father was. Patty, Scott's wife, had stopped before the ceremony at a dollar store and purchased tiaras and feather boas for all of us to wear (mimicking the prom queen). We all practiced our "wave" before the class filed into the gymnasium. The look on Megan's face when she saw us was quite memorable. We also had signs and streamers. When she walked across the stage, we could not contain ourselves. There was a huge cheer from all of us and many others in the gym. Afterwards, I apologized to the principal, and he was a good sport about the whole thing. Megan left Lansing Catholic that day, prepared to begin the next phase in her life.

We had Megan's graduation open house on June 10, 2006. It was a grand celebration. Many of Maureen and Dick's friends attended, as well as many of Megan's friends from St. Patrick's. There were also many of her former neighbors in attendance. Of course, her Lansing friends came, too. The weather was beautiful, and people stayed until late in the evening. Like many family celebrations, we didn't want it to end, and the time seemed to pass much too quickly. It was Megan's day, to honor what an amazing young woman she had become. I also celebrated and honored myself that day. I kept flashing back to Maureen's dying day and the promise I had made to her. I had done my best. I had taken "good care of Megan."

In June, 2007, Megan completed her first year in college. We missed her terribly, but at the same time, shared in her excitement as she experienced college life. She chose St. Mary's/Notre Dame as her college. She auditioned for the Notre Dame Irish Dance Team and become a proud member. In the fall of her freshman year I observed her as she came leaping through the football tunnel and onto the field at Notre Dame to do an Irish step dance with her team during a pep rally.

Megan has continued to do well academically. She made the dean's list both semesters. She has decided to pursue a career in the medical field.

In June of 2007, we also proudly watch Matthew graduate from high school with honors. He has developed his own set of talents. He is a gifted singer and was involved in the performing arts for four years in high school. He took part in eight productions. In March of 2007, he and another Lansing Catholic student were invited to sing the national anthem at Michigan State University's Breslin Center for the high school boys' basketball finals. It was certainly a proud moment for us.

In August of 2007, we became empty nesters. Matthew went off to Chicago Loyola University and Megan returned to South Bend. Matthew auditioned for the Loyola acappela team and was one of twelve chosen from a field of two hundred. Megan returned to her Notre Dame Irish Dance Team. We are thankful that both of them have flourished in their new surroundings.

And what about "Squirt," the cat that Megan begged me to take with us when we left her house more than twelve years ago? Unbelievably, he, too, is still a part of our family. After a short period of adjustment, he made himself at home and has remained an indoor cat. He has no desire to go outside. Every once in awhile, he'll venture outside when the door opens, and then he doesn't quite know what to do. He is no longer a barn cat by any stretch of the imagination. We estimate that he is at least seventeen years old.

Faith, Family, Friends

I t is clear to me that we could have not survived the past twelve years without three things: faith, family, and friends. Our faith, although sometimes greatly tested, teaches us about life and death. Although it took awhile, I made my peace with God. Someday I will find the answers to my "why" questions. For now, I have to put them aside and place my trust in God. I know that on some glorious day, I will see my dad, Dick, and Maureen again. There will be no more sadness, no more grief.

In the meantime, my prayers are simple. I thank God for the gift of every day. I pray that I will treat each day as the gift that it is, in every action that I undertake. I ask for his blessings on Megan and Matt, and to keep them safe and healthy. I pray for all those that are sick and suffering, and I pray for a cure for cancer. Of course, I also throw in a prayer for smaller, daily "issues" every now and then. My faith sustains me each and every day.

Family? Boy, what can you say about a family like mine? Many people have commented that the McGlinchey family is a special group of people. I have no doubt that we are. I remember after Maureen died, Jack took Megan aside and told her that even though none of them would try to replace her dad, from that day forward, she would have many "daddies." And indeed, Ed, Jack, Pat, Tom, and my nephews all stepped up to the plate and helped Mark be the "dad." Raising Megan became an extended family affair.

And as an extended family, we continue to have many great gatherings. We number well into the thirties now, with the great-grandchildren increasing every year. So, in every way, life goes on, and death is replaced by new life. We continue to be a very close family, and no time is like "family time." Mom and Dad, two very humble people that boarded a ship in the 1920s and left Ireland for a better life, have, indeed, created quite a legacy in America. My family sustains me each and every day.

Friends? We are blessed to have so many wonderful friends. I am thankful for my teacher friends in Eaton Rapids. When I was experiencing the worst time in my life, they were there for me in every way. We often walked at lunch, and I would tell them the latest news related to Dad, Dick, or Maureen. Often, we would have to stop, and they would literally offer me a shoulder to cry on. I'm sure there were times that they just didn't want to listen anymore, but they never let me feel as if I was a burden to them. In addition, I had my choir friends at St. Mary Cathedral. We did a lot of praying and singing together, and many of them came to the funerals of Dick and Maureen to offer support. There are just too many friends for me to mention. I am convinced, however, that we survive such trials in our life because we have the support of good friends around us. Finally, my friends help to sustain me each and every day.

Megan turned twenty in October, 2007. I continue to think about and to talk to Maureen and Dick very often, and I'm sure those discussions will continue as Megan makes her way in the world. They will have to be her guardian angels wherever she chooses to go. I'll simply have to turn her back over to their care and trust that they will take care of her when she is away from home. My relationship with them continues on a spiritual level. Whenever Megan accomplishes great things, I just say, "Hey, look at her now!" I am sure they know and can see.

This story has been about hope. In spite of everything, there is hope in the darkest of circumstances. Megan is living proof of the hope that cancer failed to steal. Twelve years ago, I could not have imagined this life of joy restored, promises kept, and dreams achieved. When all is said and done, I remain certain of one thing. During their lifetimes, Maureen and Dick blessed us with many wonderful gifts; but none were as sweet, none as endearing, as Megan, their final gift.

The legacy Mom and Dad created in America.
(with a few DeShetlers)

Cancer is so limited...
It cannot cripple Love.
It cannot shatter Hope.
It cannot corrode Faith.
It cannot destroy Peace.
It cannot kill Friendship.
It cannot suppress Memories.
It cannot silence Courage.
It cannot conquer the Spirit.
It cannot invade the Soul.
It cannot steal Eternal Life.

Author Unknown

Epilogue

Incredibly, the cancer deaths in our family did not end with Maureen. On March 14, 2003, we once again gathered at the bedside of a loved one to say goodbye. This time, it was "Lizzy," Jack's beloved wife of more than thirty years. She died of colon cancer. That same year in September, we said another goodbye to Mark's brother, Russ. He lost his battle to kidney cancer. Both were in their late fifties. In March of 2007, Scott, Jeri, and Jill lost their mother, Judy, to breast cancer. She had battled the disease courageously for several years.

We have all had too much "practice" with this disease, and I'm often drawn to reflect on the poem (left) that Scott, Jeri, and Jill included in the notes they sent after Judy's funeral. I prefer to think of it as the poem describes. I often visualize all of our loved ones, friends and relatives, in heaven having a great time together. We had many grand earthly celebrations. I'm convinced that they are now having some grand heavenly celebrations.

As time marches on, cancer still continues to devastate. It shatters our joys and disturbs our sense of peace. Cancer showed no mercy in the case of Veronica Olney, a little fifth grader at school who fought valiantly for the last three years with an insidious form of bone cancer. She died on March 17, 2008. She was *ten* years old! She was a beautiful child, a gifted student, and talented dancer. Imagine all of the dreams and hopes for the future that died with her. Imagine the devastation this has caused for her family and friends. Ten years old girls are not supposed to die of cancer.

And the struggle continues here, on earth. The word "cancer" causes a reaction of fear and trepidation for most of us. Imagine our response in October of 2007, when Megan discovered a lump in her breast. She made an appointment with our family physician, who recommended that she have an ultrasound done. Megan had the ultrasound done while she was at school in South Bend, then she came home in late October for an appointment with the breast surgeon. He did a needle biopsy on October 31. We waited for forty-eight endless hours. On November 2, we received the call that it was a fibrocystic benign tumor. Needless to say, I was extremely relieved to hear the results, but saddened that she is a <u>twenty</u> year old with this experience already in her health history. She joins a group of women with dubious distinction. We are distinct because we spend too much time wondering "if" or "when" we will get breast cancer. She is too young to worry about this.

In 1971, President Nixon declared a "war" on cancer. It seems that the progress we have made since that time has been minimal and we are losing the "war." Although people are living longer *with* cancer, the death rate for cancer remains staggering and has not substantially changed in the last thirty years.

Each day in the United States, approximately 1,500 people will lose their battle with cancer, *which means the heart-wrenching scenes described in this book will occur within families across America sixty times per hour, or every minute of every day!*

This monster has to be stopped. It steals parents away from their babies and babies away from their parents. It kills husbands and wives. It claims grandparents, aunts, uncles, nieces, nephews. Along with the person it kills, it snatches great personalities, wonderful minds, future opportunities, and, most mournfully, love. There are moments when I ache for the love of my beloved sister and all the wonderful people mentioned in this book.

My anger is now directed at the disease that took these wonderful people from me. It will take the outrage of all of us to win this "war" once and for all. We *must* do whatever it takes. Let's begin *this* war again!

Printed in the United States
129564LV00001BA/34/P